A Har

"A damned town tamer," Cordwainer muttered.

Then he looked at the three men. His gaze fell on each face in turn as his mind captured thoughts, worked them over, and formulated them into the words he was about to speak.

"Well, that makes it simple, then," Jess said. "You men know what you have to do."

"What's that?" Creek asked.

"Bushwhack Slocum any way you can. I want his damned lamp put out. Pronto."

"Well, we know where he's stayin'," Hutch said. "We can pump a couple of barrels full of buckshot through his winder and splatter him all over that hotel room."

"Be easy," Creek said.

"Don't kid yourself, Joe," Jess said. "Slocum hasn't lived this long because he's a fool. Wherever you take him down, you'd better make sure he don't get up. I've heard stories about this bastard that would curl your hair. He won't be easy."

JAKE LOGAN

SLOCUM
AND THE
GOLDEN GALS

JOVE BOOKS, NEW YORK

THE BERKLEY PUBLISHING GROUP
Published by the Penguin Group
Penguin Group (USA) Inc.
375 Hudson Street, New York, New York 10014, USA

Penguin Group (Canada), 90 Eglinton Avenue East, Suite 700, Toronto, Ontario M4P 2Y3, Canada
(a division of Pearson Penguin Canada Inc.) • Penguin Books Ltd., 80 Strand, London WC2R 0RL,
England • Penguin Group Ireland, 25 St. Stephen's Green, Dublin 2, Ireland (a division of Penguin
Books Ltd.) • Penguin Group (Australia), 250 Camberwell Road, Camberwell, Victoria 3124, Australia
(a division of Pearson Australia Group Pty. Ltd.) • Penguin Books India Pvt. Ltd., 11 Community
Centre, Panchsheel Park, New Delhi—110 017, India • Penguin Group (NZ), 67 Apollo Drive,
Rosedale, Auckland 0632, New Zealand (a division of Pearson New Zealand Ltd.) • Penguin Books
(South Africa) (Pty.) Ltd., 24 Sturdee Avenue, Rosebank, Johannesburg 2196, South Africa

Penguin Books Ltd., Registered Offices: 80 Strand, London WC2R 0RL, England

This is a work of fiction. Names, characters, places, and incidents either are the product of the author's
imagination or are used fictitiously, and any resemblance to actual persons, living or dead, business
establishments, events, or locales is entirely coincidental

SLOCUM AND THE GOLDEN GALS

A Jove Book / published by arrangement with the author

PUBLISHING HISTORY
Jove edition / September 2012

Copyright © 2012 by Penguin Group (USA) Inc.
Cover illustration by Sergio Giovine.

ISBN: 978-0-515-15108-4

JOVE®
Jove Books are published by The Berkley Publishing Group,
a division of Penguin Group (USA) Inc.,
375 Hudson Street, New York, New York 10014.
JOVE® is a registered trademark of Penguin Group (USA) Inc.
The "J" design is a trademark of Penguin Group (USA) Inc.

PRINTED IN THE UNITED STATES OF AMERICA

10 9 8 7 6 5 4 3 2 1

1

John Slocum heard the screams long before he saw the burning man.

His horse, Ferro, nickered and the gelding's ears stiffened into cones that twisted to pick up the sound.

The screams rose in pitch to a terrible shriek, and Slocum scrambled out of his bedroll and picked up his pistol and holster. He strapped on his gun belt and stooped down to scoop up his hat.

He slipped his rifle from its scabbard attached to his saddle, which was draped across a small boulder, and he ran across the road. He jacked a shell into the firing chamber of his Winchester and ran toward the screams onto Cactus Flat.

Dawn hovered above the mountains in a painted sky that was all faint pastel pink and gray clouds, their edges turning yellow gold under sprays of gauzy light.

Slocum scrambled over the rocks and skirted the prickly pear, weaved through sentinels of cedar and pinyon. Then he saw the man just as he stopped scream-ing. He was nailed, or tied, to a small juniper, and flames engulfed him and spread over the limbs like bright red and orange flags.

He heard the crackle of the dry limbs as they burned and released their gases. The man's face was black with blood boiling off his skin, melting his face as if it were made of wax. The man's arms twisted in the fire and dripped hissing fat onto the ground. His loins rippled with flame and the cloth of his trousers hissed as they turned to ash, dropped away to reveal the blackening bones of his legs.

Slocum heard the sound of hoofbeats and ducked down. He peered past the burning man and saw three riders leading a riderless saddle horse break from the trees and gallop up the road toward Halcyon Valley. He could hear their laughter as it floated on the morning air, and his jaw tightened in anger.

The smell of burning flesh was sickening and he turned away, gulped in air to keep from vomiting.

There was nothing left of the man by the time Slocum recovered from his nausea. Around the tree there was nothing to reveal his identity nor why he had been so brutally murdered. Nor had he seen a recognizable face amid the torturous flames that melted the man's flesh.

Slocum cursed under his breath, turned, and started back toward his campsite at Whiskey Springs.

That was when he heard a noise, a noise that threw him into a fighting crouch and impelled him to grasp the butt of his Colt with his right hand.

It was a man clearing his throat, or hawking up phlegm.

Slocum turned in a half circle to face the direction of the sound.

Beyond the charred corpse, he saw movement. Someone scuttled furtively amid the trees and cactus.

Slocum stood up.

"You there," he called. "You come over here or I'll drop you where you stand."

The man had frozen in place. He wore a battered hat and a frayed coat. He carried a white bundle under his arm. His pants were baggy and soiled, evident even from a distance of more than fifty yards.

The man threw both hands up in the air and his bundle dropped to the ground. It made a muffled sound, like a pillow being punched with a fist.

"Don't you shoot! Don't shoot!" the man yelled. "I ain't your enemy. I ain't no enemy."

"Pick up your bundle and walk over to me," Slocum said.

The pale ghosts of blue shadows slid from the trees as the sun rose over the mountains. A hawk sailed on silent pinions from the foothills and floated over the flat, its head shifting from side to side as it gazed downward for mice or rabbits.

The man hobbled toward Slocum, his bundle tucked again under his arm. Slocum saw the long strands of gray hair streaming from under his crumpled hat. He squeezed his bundle when it was about to slip from his grasp and it rattled like a diamondback.

"Yes, sir, here I am. Innocent as a dove and not your enemy."

Slocum pointed to the charred corpse. The man's head swiveled around to look at it. His body jerked as if he had been whipped, and he brought a hand to his mouth.

"You see what happened here?" Slocum asked.

The man looked up at him, his eyes sheepish, his lower lip atremble.

"Some of it. Yeah. I reckon. Too much of it."

"You scared?" Slocum asked.

"Plumb scared, yep. It ain't somethin' you see ever' day."

"You know who did this? There were three men who rode off. They were leading a riderless horse."

The man looked around him as if afraid of being overheard. The sound of hoofbeats had long since died away.

"Well, I seen 'em before. All four of 'em. But I didn't know none of 'em, 'ceptin' that burnt man over yonder."

"You walk down here?" Slocum asked. "And what have you got in that bundle, baby rattlesnakes?"

The man cackled and shook his head.

"No, sir, I been shakin' pinyon nuts outen them trees. I spread out this sheet and they fall there like rat shit. Mighty fine tastin' when I roast 'em."

"What's your name?"

"Caleb. Caleb Butterbean. That's who I am. I rode down here from Halcyon Valley on my mule. He's teth-ered in a draw back yonder where I was shakin' down pinyon nuts. I was real surprised when them boys rode down here and tacked Lonnie Taylor to that juniper. He was screamin' and yellin' the whole time and I didn't know they was goin' to burn him."

"Why did they do that?" Slocum asked.

"I reckon it was over some gal up in Halcyon Valley. One gal in particular, Ruby Dawson. Purty as a newborn bunny she is and, well, I guess poor Lonnie didn't listen when Jess Cordwainer told him to back off. Them three men work for Jesse and he's a bad 'un."

"Tell me more, Caleb," Slocum said. He fished a pair of cheroots from his pocket and held one out for But-terbean. "Smoke?"

"Well, that's mighty kind of you, stranger. Say, what's yore name, if you don't mind me askin'?"

"Slocum. John Slocum."

"John Slocum. Hmm. Sounds some familiar. Heard it somewheres, I reckon. You from Victorville?"

"No."

"Hesperia maybe? Barstow?"

"No, I'm not from anywhere," Slocum said.

Slocum struck a match and lit their skinny cigars. Butterbean puffed and looked up at Slocum, his forehead wrinkling and unwrinkling as if he were trying to place a man he had never seen before.

"You headed for Antelope Valley?" Butterbean asked, his mouth obscured by a wavery scarf of smoke.

"Nope," Slocum replied.

"Where you headed, then?"

"Halcyon Valley."

"Not much there, 'ceptin' a heap of trouble."

Slocum said nothing as he pulled smoke from his cheroot.

"You don't give up much, do you, Slocum?"

"Not if I don't have to," Slocum said, a thin smile curving his lips around the cigar.

"Let me get my mule over yonder and I'll ride up there with you. Pinyon pickin's ain't that good nohow."

"You got a shovel with you?"

"A small one. Why?"

"Bury that corpse yonder," Slocum said.

"Well, I reckon we could maybe dig a hole for him. You wait here. I'll get old Josie. Ah, my mule."

Slocum waited and smoked until Butterbean and Josie waddled across the flat toward him. He walked over to the burning man and began to throw loose dirt on the remaining flames. The stench of the burned body was sickly sweet and nauseating.

Butterbean dismounted and pulled a short-handled shovel from the rolled-up slicker and blanket lashed down behind the cantle of his saddle. He walked over toward Slocum, scuffing the ground with the heel of his boots. He stopped at a patch of soft earth that was not too stony nor sprouting clumps of cactus. He drove the blade of the shovel hard into the ground and grunted with satisfaction.

"This might make a good spot for poor Lonnie Taylor, God rest his soul."

Together, the two men gingerly removed the burned body from the tree. The man's eyes were boiled out and there was just a waxy white substance where they had been. His body was ravished to the bone, and they laid the skeletonized remains in the hole. Butterbean shoved dirt over him.

"One of us should probably say a few words over him," Caleb said.

"Suit yourself," Slocum said.

"You don't have nothin' to say, I take it."

"He can't hear us and I don't think any words of mine will help him. Wherever he was going, he's already there," Slocum said. "If you're going back up to Halcyon Valley, I'll meet you at the spring."

"I'll be along," Butterbean said.

He watched Slocum walk away toward Whiskey Springs and blew out a soundless whistle of air.

"Now there goes a hard man," he said to himself as he took off his hat and commended the dead man's soul to whatever heaven might exist.

2

Slocum was just pulling his single cinch tight around Ferro's belly when Butterbean rode up on his sorry mule.

"Mighty fine horse you got there, Slocum," he said.

"He'll do to ride the river with," Slocum said as he flipped down from the left stirrup. He patted his bedroll behind the cantle, felt the firmness of his shotgun wrapped inside, and stood by his horse to survey his campsite one last time.

"I brung a bottle," Caleb said. "I see you left you one under that rock yonder."

"My friend in Halcyon Valley told me that was the custom."

"Yep, that's why they call it Whiskey Springs. Folks campin' here or passin' by always leaves a full bottle of whiskey for the freighters and mail haulers. Kind of a way to show gratitude and wet a few whistles."

"It's a good custom," Slocum said as he took the

bottle of Old Grandad from Butterbean. He walked it over to the large rock beneath the talus slope of the limestone bluff and placed it a few inches from the bottle he had placed there, Old Overholt. He returned to Ferro and climbed into the saddle.

"Mighty fond of black, ain't ye?" Caleb said as the saddle creaked with the tall man's weight.

"I reckon," Slocum said. "Makes me easy to spot in daylight in case folks don't want to tangle with me, and at night, they have a hell of a time picking me out of the shadows."

Caleb chuckled.

"I got to remember that," he said. "Might come in handy someday."

The two men headed up the long winding road toward the mountains. The sun was up by then and its rays glistened off the high snow-capped peaks, bright enough to blind a man who looked at them directly.

"Who you goin' to see up in Halcyon Valley?" Caleb asked as he accepted a cheroot from Slocum. He leaned over as Slocum held a hand cupped around the flame of a lighted match.

"Wally Newman," Slocum said. "Know him?"

He couldn't be sure, but he thought that Caleb had let out a light gasp at the sound of his friend's name.

"Wallace Newman," Caleb intoned, as if he were reading a name on a tombstone.

"You know Wally?" Slocum said.

"I know he's got a big target on his back, and Cordwainer's lookin' down the barrel of a Sharps."

"You better explain that, Caleb."

"Your friend Newman was runnin' against one of Cordwainer's men for constable. Wallace claims he can clean up Halcyon Valley, get rid of the claim jumpers and bandits that have been stealin' the prospectors and miners blind. Cordwainer don't want no reforms and your friend Newman has been in hiding for two weeks with men a-huntin' him down who aim to do what they done to Lonnie Taylor, or worse."

"I know Wally's been prospecting," Slocum said. "I didn't know he was a politician."

"Wally, I hear, has a mine where he struck a heavy vein or maybe a mother lode and don't nobody know where it's at. That's another reason he's got hard men on his tail."

"In Halcyon Valley?" Slocum said.

The two men climbed up toward the lavender sky where the air thinned and the sun slid over the high peaks, spraying a golden mist over Cactus Flat. The hills were more rugged there and the road grew steeper.

"Tell me about this Ruby gal. Where does she fit in?"

"Ruby hands out love like it was sugar candy, but Cordwainer has a hold on her. He thinks. She runs a brothel for him, but she grants favors to men he don't know about. Oh, she's a whizbang, that one. Your friend Wally got tangled up with her, I hear, but she was just tryin' to find out where his gold mine is. He dropped her, wisely, but she's one determined bitch. Or so I hear."

"You think she's sweet on Wally?"

Caleb shrugged.

"Could be, but Cordwainer don't want him killed until he finds that mine."

"Can't Cordwainer find out from the register where Wally recorded his claim?"

"That's just it. Nobody can find his claim. Not in San Bernardino or Los Angeles. I figger he recorded his claim maybe up in Sacramento and maybe under a different name."

They topped a rise and rode toward a dry lake with a wooden structure at one end of it. The lake bed was mottled white, dry as a bone.

"Lake Ettinger," Caleb said. "That's his mine up there. In spring, the lake is full of water, but when it's dry, like now, you can see the cyanide Ettinger uses to separate the gold from the ore they bring out of his mine."

"It looks abandoned," Slocum said.

"Well, it ain't. Barney Ettinger is a millionaire from Los Angeles. He says there's a lake of pure gold underneath Halcyon Valley. That mine of his is burrowing a tunnel straight under the valley. It's slow work and tedious as hell, but he's finding veins of gold somewhere down in them rocks."

"I thought all the gold was taken out up at Sutter's Mill."

Caleb's laugh was a scratchy cackle.

"'Bout ten, eleven years ago, a feller named Rick Hammond come up here from Grizzly Lake and saw a promisin' piece of limestone. He took some dynamite sticks and blasted a big old hole in the outdroppin'. He found some big chunks of gold, and when he went to the assay office down in San Bernardino, the word got out and folks streamed up to the valley and started pannin' and diggin'. Gold petered out and folks left the valley. Now that Ettinger's up here, more prospectors are pokin' around. That's when your friend Wally come up, 'bout two year ago, and struck it rich. Ha. A lot of good it did him. He's a marked man, for shore."

"He didn't tell me about his mine," Slocum said. "Just that he was in trouble and needed help."

"Did he tell you he owns a hotel in Halcyon Valley?"

"Yeah. He's got a room waiting for me at that hotel, The Excelsior."

"Yep, he owns it and his sister, Abigail, runs it. Pretty little thing, but smart as a whip."

"She was just a young girl when I last saw her. Little Abby."

"Well, she's a full-blown woman now and drives off the men like they was a herd of moonin' calves. She don't take kindly to the rough old boys who want to spark her."

They rode past the Ettinger mine and down a tree-lined road into thick woods. The woods opened up into a large valley with signs of life. There was a main street and at least two hotels, a small bank, a constable's office and jail, a grocery store next to an arrastre, where a mule was circling as the ore was being crushed in a large round hole. Men stood around, smoking and talking. But they all stared at Butterbean and Slocum as they rode in. They passed one hotel, the Polygon House, a crazy structure of angles and wings that seemed slapped together with whipsawed lumber by a drunken carpenter. Farther down the street was The Excelsior, which was square and almost staid by contrast, with three floors, and a porch with chairs and benches occupied by two elderly women and three whiskered and bearded men smoking pipes.

"Well, there you are, John. I hope you know what you're gettin' into. Town looks pretty tame now, but at night, the two saloons are lit up and the whiskey is flowin' and you can get into a game of cards or a fistfight."

"I don't see any saloons," Slocum said as they rode up to the hitch rail in front of the hotel.

"Over in them trees yonder is one, the Hoot Owl, and at the other end of Main Street is the other'n, the Jubilee."

"Where do you bunk, Caleb?"

"I got me a little shack over beyond that big juniper on the edge of town. See it? That 'un with the double trunks." Caleb pointed.

"I see it."

"That's the hangin' tree, John. Many a man has had his neck stretched from that big ol' limb that shoots out from the trunk."

Slocum had a queasy feeling when he looked at the twin limbs of the large juniper. He rubbed his neck as if to reassure himself that he had no rope around it.

"It looks peaceful enough now," he said.

"Just an illusion. They hung a boy from that juniper just last week. Stole a horse, he did, and they caught him down in Grizzly Lake."

Slocum wondered what he was getting into as he looked once more at the sleepy little settlement. Maybe it came to life when the sun went down. He was not sure what kind of life there would be, but the town was right in the middle of a beautiful valley surrounded by green, pine-studded hills.

He wondered what Wally wanted him to do. He was not a hired gun, and was himself a wanted man, back in Georgia, wrongly accused of murdering a judge.

"See you, Caleb," Slocum said as he dismounted and wrapped his reins around the hitch rail.

"I'll be at the Hoot Owl tonight. I'll buy you a drink and bring some of these roasted pinyon nuts."

"That would be fine. We'll see."

Caleb leaned over and spoke to Slocum in a low tone of voice.

"I been thinkin', John," he said. "'Bout Wallace registerin' his mine. You might be lettin' the cat out of the bag by comin' up here."

"What do you mean?" Slocum asked.

"Maybe Wallace registered his mine under your name."

"Where did you get that, Caleb?"

"Well, I knowed they checked for Abigail's name and Wally's widder's name, Lorelei, and anybody else he knows up here. But nobody knows about you yet and my bet is he used your name. You may be the owner of a gold mine and not even know it."

"I'll ask Wally when I see him," Slocum said and touched two fingers to his hat brim in a sign of farewell.

Caleb rode off toward the double-trunked juniper, the hanging tree.

3

Slocum lifted his saddlebags free of Ferro's back, pulled his rifle from its sheath, and walked up the stairs to the hotel porch. He left his bedroll with the sawed-off shotgun lashed to the horse's rump behind the cantle.

As his boots struck the porch, one of the women lifted her fan, folded it, and waved him to approach. Slocum walked over to her. The other people on the porch bent their necks to hear what the woman had to say.

"Young man," the jowly woman with the silvery hair said, "may I ask you a question?"

"Why, sure, ma'am," Slocum said.

"Did you just ride in from Victorville?"

"I passed through there yesterday," he said.

"We wonder if you might have seen our grandson, Lorenzo Taylor. People here told us he rode to Victorville. But we were supposed to meet him here yesterday."

Slocum felt something grip his heart and squeeze it.

His stomach swirled with a minor queasiness as he thought about the man burned to death down on Cactus Flat.

"We call him 'Lonnie,'" one of the old men called across the porch. "Said he wanted us to meet his betrothed. Planned on marrying a woman he met up here in Halcyon Valley."

The old man had a bald pate bordered by slabs of white hair, which gave him the look of an albino sheep dog.

The other man leaned forward in his chair and added his comment. Slocum felt hemmed in by old folks.

"He told us the name of his bride-to-be, Ruby Dawson. She told us Lonny had to go to Victorville, but that's a long ways for us after our trip from Los Angeles by stage."

"Did you see a young man riding to Victorville?" asked the other matron, who was fanning away gnats that buzzed around her perfumed head of bluish hair, which seemed to have been plastered on with pomade.

"No, ma'am, I didn't," Slocum said. "Nobody was on the trail from Victorville when I rode through yesterday."

The faces of the people on the porch fell and he could see that they were disappointed. But he hadn't lied to them. He never saw their grandson on the trail because he was being nailed to a tree and set afire. He didn't have the heart to tell them they would never see Lonnie Taylor again. Not in this life.

"I'm sorry," he said, and walked toward the heavy doors of the hotel. He heard them all chattering as he entered the hotel and kicked the door shut behind him.

The old carpet had pathways worn into it, faint but visible to his trail-practiced eye. Off to his right was a small dining room. The aroma of cooked beef and bacon drifted through the opening, and out of the corner of his eye, he saw the flickering silhouettes of early diners, steam rising from their coffee cups, sunlight streaming through glasses of water like vaporous mists. He walked to the desk and cleared his throat as he leaned his rifle against the outer wall next to a potted plant with shiny green leaves.

A young man appeared in a doorway behind the counter. He wore a black vest and a striped white shirt with a garter belt around the right sleeve just above his elbow. He was short and thin, with deep-sunk eyes bracketing a slightly aquiline nose. His upper lip was bristling with the sandy fuzz of a beginning mustache, which barely matched the thick tawny hair sprouting in unruly spikes in several directions on his head, as if they'd erupted out of his skull then frozen solid. Yes, sir," the young man said. "Do you wish a room?"

Slocum looked down at the young man, whom he judged to be no more than eighteen or nineteen. A slight smile curled his lips.

"If you have one reserved for me, son. I'm John Slocum."

The young man's mouth opened, and he blinked his pale blue eyes. His Adam's apple bobbed as he swallowed his own slight trickle of saliva.

From the dining room came the tinkle of eating utensils clinking against plates and the tiny ringing sounds of water glasses jostling together on trays. The overstuffed furniture in the lobby gave off a musty odor, which clashed with the warm scents of coffee and cooked food.

The young man opened the ledger on the counter and turned it around. He lifted a pen from a small inkwell and proffered it to Slocum.

"Yes, sir, there is a room reserved for you, Mr. Slocum. If you'll just make your mark on the empty line just below the last signature, you're on the first floor, really one of the nicest rooms we have, with a back entrance at the end of the hall. And we have a livery stable two hunnert yards behind the hotel, just a little ways into the woods."

"I'll find it," Slocum said as he signed the guest register. "Miss Abby around?"

"She don't come in till nigh noon."

"What's your name, son?"

"Samuel Davis. Folks call me Sammy."

"All right, Sammy. If you'll give me a key, I think I can find my room."

Sammy went to the sidewall and took a skeleton key off a metal hook. The key had a tag on it with the room number. He handed it to Slocum.

"Last room down the hall, on your right, Mr. Slocum."

"Thanks." Slocum scraped the key off the counter and hefted his rifle.

"I'll tell Miss Abby you're here when she comes in," Sammy said as Slocum walked toward the hallway next to the stairs.

Slocum said nothing, but continued down the hall to his room, number 6. He unlocked the door and went in. He tossed his rifle and bedroll on top of the bed and walked to the window. It looked out over bare ground and into woods. The woods were mostly pine, with a few spruce and fir mixed in. He saw the log structure through the trees, parts of it, and decided that was where the stable was, just out of sight.

The room had a table and two chairs, and a mirrored bureau with a washbowl and a porcelain pitcher sitting atop a doily. Two water glasses had been provided. To his surprise, a bottle of Kentucky bourbon also sat in front of the small mirror. There was a note stuck under its bottom.

"Make yourself at home, Johnnie," the note read. It was signed "Abby," and there were X's and O's beneath her name.

Slocum smiled.

Abby had always called him Johnnie. He hadn't seen her since she was in pigtails, but he remembered her freckled face, her bright eyes, and her politeness when he'd visited Wally in Texas before Wally's wife, Lorelei, died. She and Wally had raised Abby after the accidental deaths of his parents, then he took care of his little sister by himself after the death of his wife.

Slocum left the room, locked it, and walked down the hall to the lobby.

Sammy hailed him from behind the check-in counter.

The young man held a piece of paper in his hand.

"Oh, Mr. Slocum, if you're going to the livery, here's a chit. You give that to Alvaro and he'll put up your horse, feed him, and curry him. All paid for by Miss Abby."

Slocum took the slip of paper and slid it into his shirt pocket.

"Thanks, Sammy," he said.

"You must be real important, Mr. Slocum. This is the first time I seen Miss Abby give out a free room and pay for boarding your horse."

"Just you see you keep me out of your conversations, Sammy. Otherwise, you could come to harm."

Sammy gulped and his face paled.

"My lips is sealed, Mr. Slocum," he whispered loudly.

Slocum smiled and walked across the empty lobby,

his boots muffled by the carpet, the sound of them absorbed by the overstuffed furniture. The porch was empty, too, as he stepped outside, and the only sound he heard was the grinding of rocks in the arrastre as the mule walked in a circle, hitched to the wooden flange like some creature in perpetual bondage.

Slocum mounted Ferro and rode to the next street and turned to the right. He rode along the fringe of woods, the scent of juniper, pinyon, and pine strong in his nostrils. He found the stable and saw that it and the corrals had all been constructed with logs and the place reeked of horse droppings, hay, corn, and horse sweat.

He dismounted in front of the double doors and led Ferro inside the large structure, where the smells were even stronger. He stopped just inside and looked back out toward the rear of The Excelsior Hotel.

A man stood on tiptoe and was peering into the window of Slocum's hotel room. He stood there for several seconds, shading his eyes with one hand. He wore a strapped-down holster with a hogleg jutting from it and a belt crammed with the glistening brass of .45-caliber cartridges.

Slocum's mind flashed back to that morning when he had seen three men ride off from Cactus Flat. This man, with his faded red shirt and denim trousers, had been one of those men.

No mistake.

Slocum watched as the man turned away from the hotel window and entered the building through the back door.

He wondered if Sammy's lips were sealed. He'd bet money that the clerk had shown the man the hotel register with his name scrawled on the last line.

He had written, "John Slocum, Laramie, Wyoming."

A voice came out of the darkness of the barn.

"That man you look at, he is called Hutch," said the voice with a Spanish accent. "He is a bad man. He is a killer. He is very dangerous."

"Do you know who I am?" Slocum asked.

"No, I do not know you, but I see the dust on your horse and you look tired. It is one dollar a day to board your horse, four bits more for grain or hay, and another four bits if you wish me to curry him."

"If you're Alvaro, Sammy gave me this chit to give you."

The man walked over and Slocum handed him the slip of paper.

"I am Alvaro Cardona," he said as he read the scrawl on the paper. "Yes, sir, I have been expecting you, even though I do not know how you are called."

"Me llamo John Slocum," he said in Spanish.

Alvaro grinned and held out his hand.

"Mucho gusto en conocerlo," he said, and Slocum knew he had made a new friend.

Alvaro took the reins from Slocum's hand and led Ferro to a water trough near the rear entrance.

As Ferro bent his neck to drink, Alvaro began to loosen the saddle cinch while he patted the horse's neck.

"I will take care of this fine animal," Alvaro said as Slocum walked up and stood near him.

Then Alvaro turned and looked at Slocum.

"Ten cuidado con Hutch," he said in liquid Spanish.

Slocum understood him all too well.

Beware of Hutch.

4

The three men were eating breakfast in the dining hall of the Polygon House when they saw Butterbean ride by on his mule. There was another man, dressed in black and riding a black horse, riding into town with him.

"There's that old bastard Butterbean," Cory Windom said.

"Yeah, I'll bet that bastard was shakin' pinyon nuts out of the trees down in Cactus Flat when we burned Lonnie Taylor," Joe Creek said. "He'd better keep his mouth shut if he seen us."

"Who's the jasper with him?" Allen Hutchins asked. He was the man they called Hutch. "He shore don't look like no prospector to me."

The three men looked Slocum over with keen eyes narrowed to slits.

"He looks like a gunslick to me," Creek said.

"What in hell would he be wantin' up here?" Cory asked. "Hutch, you better foller him, see where he goes."

"I ain't finished my breakfast yet," Hutch complained.

"All right, I'll tell Cordwainer you was too busy stuffin' your damned craw to check on that pilgrim what just rode by."

Hutch shoved his plate to one side and got up.

"I'll eat a big lunch," he said, glaring at Cory. "One thing about a town this small, that tall drink of water can't go fur."

Cory and Creek both laughed and continued to shovel fried eggs and beefsteak into their mouths.

Hutch walked out of the dining hall and left the lobby of the Polygon. He saw Butterbean ride off on his mule, after the man on the black horse had wrapped his reins around the hitch rail and ascended the porch steps.

Hutch kept to the shadows as he walked down the street, his eyes on the tall stranger who was talking to the old folks on the hotel porch.

He waited outside the hotel until he saw the stranger leave several minutes later after the people on the porch got up and went back inside the hotel. He stood in the shadows between the assay office and a store that sold mining tools, Abercrombie's. Abercrombie was a snaky little man who made more money than the prospectors and reported his sales to Cordwainer, as did the clerk in the assay office.

After the stranger rode off, Hutch entered the hotel and looked at the register without asking Sammy. He saw the name and asked where Slocum was rooming.

Sammy told him.

"You keep your mouth shut about this, kid," Hutch said. "I was never here."

"No, you were never here," Sammy said, his voice trembling. He knew who Hutch was and he knew what he could do to people who crossed him.

Hutch went around to the back of the hotel and looked into Slocum's room. He saw the rifle, saddlebags, and bedroll on the bed.

When he returned to the Polygon House, his companions were in the lobby, smoking hand-rolled cigarettes.

"What did you find out, Hutch?" Windom asked. His long legs were stretched out full length. His face was stippled with two days of stubble, and the scar across his nose was like a small river in the sand of his suntanned face.

"The man checked into the Excelsior, took a room at the back. He rode off but I seen his name in the register."

"Who is he?" Joe Creek asked. He blew a ghostly smoke ring into the still air of the lobby and squinted as the tail stung his ochre eyes, which straddled a button nose. He was short and stocky, with arm muscles bulging out his shirtsleeves and his neck staving off the wrinkled collar of his chambray shirt as if it were about to burst out of his clothes and leave them in shreds.

"The name he signed in the hotel register was John Slocum," Hutch said.

Cory stiffened as if he had been drenched with a pitcher full of ice water.

"Mean anything to you, Cory?" Hutch asked.

Cory stubbed his cigarette out in a clay ashtray. His expression turned sour.

"I seen a dodger on someone with that name. Wanted

for murder someplace in the South. Seems like it was in New Mexico."

"Register had him hailing from Laramie," Hutch said.

Joe Creek leaned forward in his wicker chair. The chair creaked as his weight shifted.

"Slocum," he said, as if to try out the name himself, see if it jogged his memory. "Seems like I heard his name, too, down Texas way. Horse trader who left some waddies shot dead down in Abilene."

"He's a gunslick all right," Cory said.

"We'd better tell Cordwainer who he's got in town," Joe Creek said.

"I wonder what in hell he wants up here," Windom said in a musing tone of voice.

"Maybe somebody sent for him," Creek said.

"Gun for hire? Could be," Windom said.

"Yeah, but who?" asked Hutch.

"That ain't hard to figger," Creek said. "He rode straight by here to The Excelsior. Who owns that hotel?"

Both Cory and Hutch uttered the name at the same time.

"Wally Newman."

Creek nodded in agreement.

"And Abby runs the hotel, Newman's high-and-mighty sister," he said.

"We better get over to Jess's cabin and tell him." Hutch shifted his weight as the two men rose from their chairs.

"Yeah, that Abby gal don't know Slocum's in town yet. She don't come to the hotel until nigh noon." Windom started for the doors, patted his full belly, and belched.

Creek farted loudly.

Hutch fanned his face to wipe away the sudden odor of expelled gas.

"Joe, you reek of coal oil. You blow once more, you're liable to bust into flames." Windom made a show of waving away the putrid fumes.

All three men laughed as they stomped down the steps to their horses at the hitch rail.

"What do we do with Lonnie's horse?" Hutch asked.

"Take him with us to Cordwainer's," Windom said. "Tell him what we done with Lonnie."

"He'll probably take the horse up on a bluff and shoot it," Creek said. "Jess's hate goes real deep."

"We could sell it and the tack and maybe split the money," Hutch said.

"Leave the nag here, then," Windom said. "We still got to see Jess."

The three men slipped their reins from the rail and mounted their horses.

They rode past the hanging tree and headed toward the edge of Union Flat, where Cordwainer had a small cabin surrounded by piles of large smooth boulders. During the war, the miners and prospectors chose sides and the Union sympathizers built their shelters on Union Flat. Most of the cabins were deserted now, which was the way Cordwainer liked it.

They rode through deep woods in the shade of pines as the sun climbed to its zenith.

"I'm still hungry," Hutch complained as they spotted the boulders guarding Cordwainer's house.

"Tighten your belt," Creek said.

"Maybe Jess will give you a bear claw," Windom cracked.

"Haw," exclaimed Hutch in derision. "He wouldn't give me the sweat off his balls."

"Nobody would," Windom said as they approached the log cabin at a walk.

They knew Jess's place was guarded, and if they weren't recognized, they'd all be blown out of their saddles.

The thought made Hutch's skin crawl and the hairs on the back of his neck stiffen into wire bristles.

"Hello, the house," Creek called out when they cleared the jumble of boulders. He raised a hand and waved at an unseen guard.

"Ya'll ride on up," a voice called from a clump of pines.

Cordwainer came out of the cabin and stood on the porch. He wore a Colt .45 on his hip and stood over six feet tall. He was square-shouldered and square-jawed, a man nearing forty who was as lean as a whip, all muscle with eyes brown as roasted coffee beans and flaring sideburns that matched his neatly trimmed mustache.

"You boys better have some good news for me," he said as the three men rode up to the hitch rail at the side of the cabin.

"We got good news and bad," Windom said.

Cordwainer's eyes narrowed with suspicion, but he said nothing.

He waited there on the porch listening to the creak of leather as the men dismounted. He watched them walk toward him, their boots crunching on the gravel and pine needles that glistened auburn in the pale sunlight.

The men stopped and stared up at their boss.

"Give me the good news first, Cory," Cordwainer said. "And it had better be damned good."

Hutch felt a shiver run up and down his spine as he stood in the shade of a tall pine. He could still smell the coal oil on his hands and smell the burning flesh of Lonnie Taylor. His half-empty stomach roiled with a sloshing lake of sour bile.

5

Abby Newman began to stack the groceries she had brought from town on her brother's table. She had left Halcyon Valley before dawn and ridden a circuitous route to her brother's hideout cabin above Jackrabbit Valley. She had stopped often to make sure she hadn't been followed.

"I hate to see you have to do all this for me, Abby," Wally said. "You have enough on your hands running the hotel."

"I don't mind, Wally," she assured him as she put a can of peaches next to a sack of flour. "I put out posters where I could yesterday. Had them printed in Grizzly Lake. I hope you get elected to constable come November."

"It's a long shot," he said, "but maybe I can run out Cordwainer and his cronies if I get the job."

"You'll get the job," she said. "People in town are getting fed up with Jess. I'm fed up with him. The miners

31

and the prospectors are paying him protection money and they don't like it one bit."

She took off her bonnet, sighed, and pulled out a chair and sat down. Her brother started putting the canned goods, coffee, flour, sugar, and tobacco into the kitchen cupboards, which he had made himself after building the log cabin up in the rocks above Dead Horse Canyon.

"Any sign of Slocum yet?" he asked. "John is my only hope of getting Jess Cordwainer off my back."

"No. How's the mine? Ruben working there today?"

"Thank God for Ruben Vallejo and Elisando Gonzalez. I took some gold down to Victorville yesterday. Elisando works on the arrastre and in the laboratory. Ruben is filling up the ore carts with rocks that just shine with gold."

"Wally, when will you quit? You work too hard."

He looked at his sister as he closed the cupboard door.

Abby was a delicate flower, with her mother's sea blue eyes and dark hair. Her locks flowed over her shoulders and cascaded down her back. She was slender and small, with the figure of a young girl, although she was almost twenty.

He sat down in a chair facing her across the table.

Wally was lean and muscular from hard-rock mining. His face was open and honest with brown eyes that reflected love and tenderness when he looked at Abby, as he did now. He was only five foot nine, but to her, he was as tall as any man. His short sideburns masked the scars left by forceps when he was born back in Ohio, some thirty-two years ago.

Abby's facial expression became waxen as she looked away from her brother and twirled one of the ringlets of hair that dangled in front of her right ear. It was a habit he recognized. She only did this when she was troubled, or had something weighing heavily on her mind. Her eyes clouded up as she stared out a window, lost in deep thought.

Wally reached across the table and stroked the back of Abby's hand. It was a soothing touch and yet she pulled her hand away as if it had been scorched.

"What's troubling you, sis?" he asked quietly.

"Nothing," she said quickly. Too quickly.

"Cordwainer still trying to court you?"

"Yes, but that's not it," she said. "He's persistent and he's a pest."

"Then, what is it?"

"It—it's that Ruby. Ruby Dawson."

"She's nothing but a—"

"I know what she is," Abby snapped.

"Then you shouldn't have anything to do with her, Abby."

"She's been coming around. Trying to be friendly. I am polite to her, but she keeps after me."

"To do what?" he asked.

Abby's eyes filled with mist. She wasn't crying, but she was fighting back tears.

"Do you really want to know, Wally?"

"Of course I want to know. What is she ragging you about?"

"It's all so horrible. Just to think of it."

"Go ahead, Abby," he said. "We should have no secrets between us."

She drew in a breath as if steeling herself to say what was bothering her.

"She offered me a thousand dollars to come and work for her at the Polygon House."

"What?" Wally was aghast.

"She—she said I could make a lot of money just to be friendly with the saloon patrons. Just sit at their tables and be affectionate. She said . . ."

Wally waited while his sister composed herself.

Abby pulled hard on the ringlet and her eyes filled with shadows. She looked sad and angry at the same time.

"She said that I was wasting my time at our hotel and she could make me rich."

Wally sucked in a breath.

"What did you say to her?" he asked.

"She pulled a bunch of double eagles—gold double eagles—from her purse and stacked them on the table in front of me. 'That's one thousand dollars,' she said. 'All yours. No strings attached. Money to keep. Money you don't have to pay back.'"

"The devil's temptress," Wally said.

"I got up and walked away, but I can't get those double eagles out of my mind."

"Abby, I can shower you with twenty-dollar gold pieces. You don't need Ruby's filthy money."

"I know," she said. "I told Ruby to leave the hotel and not to bother me again. I told her I would never work for her. For any amount of money."

"Good for you, sis," he said. He patted her hand and this time she did not pull it away. "Ruby and Jess want to corrupt Halcyon Valley. They are greedy and evil."

"Wally, I don't know how much more of this I can take. Jess and Ruby are so persistent. I know what they are, but they hide behind their smiles and their pretended kindness and niceness. I get mad at them, but they just act pleasant and sweet, as if they were my friends."

"You know what they really want, don't you?"

Abby shook her head.

"They want to find my mine and jump my claim. They think they can go through you and you'll tell them what they want to know."

"I guess I know that. Deep down. Oh, Wally, you have to hide from them. Cordwainer will kill you and . . ."

"Now, now, Abby. That's why I asked John Slocum to come up here. He's the only man I know who can stand up to a thieving tyrant like Cordwainer. John will know what to do, and he will help us. I trust him."

"I barely remember him," she said.

"He's a good man. You bring him here and he'll know what to do. I can't keep hiding from Cordwainer forever. Sooner or later, he'll find out about this cabin and discover my mine. His men are out hunting me every day."

"I know," she said. Then she stood up. "I'd better get back to town and take care of business at the hotel."

"And wait for Slocum," he said, rising from his chair.

"I hope he comes soon," she said.

"He'll be here."

"Good-bye, Wally," she said.

He wrapped his arms around her and squeezed her tight. "Don't worry," he said as he released her. "And be careful."

Abby picked up the oversized saddlebags next to the door and carried them out to her horse, secured them behind the cantle, and mounted the dun gelding.

Wally watched her ride away and his heart filled with a deep sadness.

"As soon as I find that mother lode," he said to himself, "I'll take us both far away from this place."

He said it to himself, but he meant it. He knew the mother lode was somewhere in the valley and he was pretty sure he could find it.

That was what kept him going. That and his love and concern for his younger sister.

6

Alvaro, curious, saw Slocum staring at the back of the hotel. He also saw the man peering in the window of the room in the rear.

"Ah," he said to Slocum, "already they are wondering who you are, Mr. Slocum."

"You know that man, Alvaro?"

Alvaro nodded. "I know who he is. He is called Allen Hutchins, but they also call him Hutch. He is a bad man. A very bad man."

"I know," Slocum said. Then he walked away from Alvaro.

"Where do you go?" Alvaro asked.

Slocum didn't answer. Hutch had gone through the back door of the hotel. Slocum ran to the front of the hotel, passing between the hotel and a wooden building. As he reached the street, he saw Hutch descending the porch stairs. He followed the man to the other hotel in town, the Polygon House, and saw him enter.

Slocum waited in the narrow shaded corridor between the hotel and a small mercantile store where he
could not be seen. He stuck a cheroot in his mouth, but
did not light it. He was a patient man and would wait
all day if need be. There were four horses tied to the
hitch rail in front of the hotel. One of them, he surmised,
had belonged to the man he had seen burn to death down
on Cactus Flat. The other three horses belonged to the
three killers who had performed the dastardly deed.
Sooner or later, the men would emerge and ride their
horses somewhere. Perhaps they would report his presence to Cordwainer. Or maybe they would ride to one
of the saloons. The town was small. He could follow on
foot if they went to either place.

He did not have to wait long.

The three men emerged from the hotel and walked
to the hitch rail. Slocum heard them argue about what
to do with Lonnie Taylor's horse. He was relieved when
they rode off and left the dead man's saddled horse for
his benefit.

He kept the men in his sight as he walked to the rail
and unwrapped the reins of the sorrel gelding with the
white stockings. He climbed into the saddle and followed his quarry at a safe distance. The three horses
kicked up dust and he was able to follow the riders past
the hanging tree and over the valley to a pine forest.

He halted when the three men approached massive
piles of huge boulders. He saw them stop and hail the
house nestled just beyond in the thick growth of tall
pine trees. They rode on and Slocum angled the sorrel
to a cluster of junipers, spruce, and fir trees within ear-
shot. He saw a man come on to the porch and, hearing
what they all said, determined that he was looking at
Jess Cordwainer.

The three men entered the house and Slocum waited, patting the withers of Taylor's horse to keep him calm.

After a time, he realized he could learn no more by staying there, so he looked up at the sun and got his bearings so that he could ride back into town and return the horse to the hotel where he had found it.

He rode back on a different route so that he could learn more about the lay of the land. The sun streamed its rays down through the woods and he felt like he was riding through an ancient cathedral with its panes of stained glass. It was peaceful and quiet.

Suddenly, the sorrel pricked its ears and Slocum saw them twist to pick up sounds. The horse's rubbery nostrils flexed as it turned its head to catch scents somewhere in the thick of the pine forest.

He peered in the direction of the horse's attentive gaze and saw a shadow moving through the columns of light. A horse and rider moved very slowly along a trackless stretch. Soon, he heard the soft crunch of iron hooves on dried pine needles, the crackle of a branch. The rider moved into a clearing and hauled in on the reins. The horse stopped as the rider looked around. Slocum patted the sorrel's withers, but the horse whickered. The rider looked straight at him, and he saw that it was a young woman.

She wore a small pistol, possibly a Smith and Wesson .38. She drew it from her holster and pointed it at Slocum.

"You there," she said. "Ride up real slow so's I can see your face. One funny move and I'll fire. I'm a crack shot."

Slocum ticked the horse's flanks with his spurs and rode at a slow walk toward the woman with the pistol.

She looked calm and her arm was steady as she held

the pistol chest high with both hands and lined him up in its sights.

"Don't shoot, ma'am. I'm just out for a ride."

He got to within fifty yards of her when she took one hand from her gun's grip and held it up flat to halt him.

"Just stay right there, mister," she said. "I recognize that horse. What are you doing on Lonnie Taylor's horse? Did you steal it from him?"

"No, ma'am," Slocum said. "I just borrowed it. Lonnie Taylor's dead."

He heard the young woman utter a gasp and her flat hand closed around the butt of her pistol once again.

"Ride up to that dab of sunlight about ten feet from me and then stop," the woman said. "I want to see your face."

Slocum eased the sorrel up to the spot indicated by the woman with the pistol. There was a circle of light that came from the sun's position overhead. He tipped his hat back on his head so that she could see his face.

"Satisfied?" he said, a sarcastic twist to the question.

"Johnnie? Is that you?"

He looked at the woman more closely. He had been staring at the .38 in her hands. Now he examined her face, partially shaded by the trees. But then she moved a foot or two closer and her face lit up as if illuminated by a bright candle.

And nobody called him "Johnnie."

Except one person. A little girl, the sister of his friend, Wally Newman.

"Abby?" he said. "Little Abby?"

Abby laughed.

"Not so little anymore, Johnnie. I've been expecting you. I just left Wally. He's anxious to see you."

She eased the hammer of her pistol back down to

half-cock and holstered it. Slocum rode up, leaned over, and gave her a hug.

"Yeah, you have grown a mite," he said, smelling the perfume in her hair, the scent of her like a fine wine in his nostrils.

Abby laughed.

"Did you get a room at our hotel?" she asked when he sat back tall in his saddle.

"Yes. Haven't had a chance to settle in yet."

"What happened to Lonnie Taylor?" she asked as she patted her hair on the side facing Slocum.

"You might not want to know. You headed back to town?"

"Yes. I just took Wally some groceries. He's hiding from men who want to find his mine and jump his claim."

"Cordwainer," he said.

"Yes," she said, a bitter tone to her voice. "Ride with me back to the hotel?"

"Sure," he said.

They rode off into the woods. She zigzagged over a course he couldn't define. She stopped often to listen and look. He watched her and saw a determined woman who was trail savvy. They saw no one, heard nothing out of the ordinary.

"I want to hear about Lonnie," she said after a few minutes of silence. "I tried to warn him about Ruby Dawson, but he wouldn't listen. Did Cordwainer kill him?"

"I think he may have ordered his death," Slocum said. "Can't prove it, but I just tracked three men who killed Taylor. They wound up at Cordwainer's."

"On Union Flat," she said. "His house is very well protected and not easy to find."

"You've been there?"

She laughed.

"I tracked him once, out of curiosity, and saw where he lived. A very secretive and devious man."

"The more I hear about him, the more I don't like him," Slocum said.

"Now tell me about Lonnie. Did they shoot him or torture him? Ruby is Jess Cordwainer's gal and Lonnie made a play for her. I think she led him on. I wouldn't trust her any more than I would trust Cordwainer and his bunch."

Slocum told her about camping at Whiskey Springs and hearing a man scream. When he described what he saw on Cactus Flat, a man tied to a tree and burning up, she cringed and he thought he saw a tear run down her cheek.

"How horrible," she said when he had finished. "I'm glad you and Caleb buried him. But now his life is in danger."

"I'm supposed to see him tonight," he said. "At the Hoot Owl Saloon."

"You tell Caleb he'd better watch his back. And you'd better do the same. Cordwainer's men go to that same saloon," she said. "And now they know who you are."

"Your clerk, Sammy, must have shown Hutch my name in the register."

"He probably had no choice. Johnnie, these are dangerous men. You know Wally. He's not a coward, but he has gone to a great deal of trouble to hide his mine from Cordwainer and he knows he's outnumbered. That's why he sent for you. He said you'd know what to do."

"I hope that's true," Slocum said.

They came to the fringe of the town. They could hear

the oval arrastre grinding, as well as the snatches of conversation from the prospectors gathered around it.

"Tomorrow, I'll take you out to see Wally. He's anxious to talk to you."

"I'm anxious to see him."

She reached over as they approached a road that encircled the town. She touched the back of his hand.

"I want you to have dinner with me tonight," she said. "In my private suite at the hotel. We can talk about old times."

"And probably about what's going on here in Halcyon Valley," he said.

"It promises to be a long evening," she said.

And Slocum wondered if there was more behind that statement than just talk.

The more he encountered women, he thought, the less he knew about what they were really thinking. He had last seen Abby when she was in pigtails and wearing black patent leather shoes. Now she was a grown woman and seemed to possess all the wiles of her sex without being blatant about it.

Abby had more of her shrewd mother in her than either her father, Whit, or her brother, Wally.

It promised to be an interesting supper, he thought, with more than food to devour.

7

Jess Cordwainer knew two things for sure. The first was that most people were stupid, and the men he hired to work for him were only slightly less stupid than the men he preyed upon. The second, which he had learned early in life, was that it was better to be a leader than a follower.

There was another facet of his character he kept hidden from most of the world. This was a secret belief that he never discussed with anyone else, because he was a man without a conscience. He did not care about people. He did not care about their feelings. He had no truck with sorrow or grief. He wasn't sorry about anything, and he had never grieved for anyone or anything.

That secret Jess bore was his conviction that he had the right to kill anyone who stood in his way, threatened him, or did not bow to his wishes.

Now, as he listened to Hutch, Joe, and Cory, he kept his anger in check. But his mind was racing like a whirlwind across a flaming prairie, burning inside him with the intensity of a blowtorch.

The three men sat on a handmade sofa covered with a thick pair of bearskins. His cabin was rustic, but boasted hardwood floors and animal skins that softened his footfalls, the hides of wolf, cougar, buffalo, deer, and elk. This was his own world, well protected and guarded by those lesser men he dominated and controlled.

When he heard Hutch utter the name *John Slocum*, his eyes narrowed to thin slits with a gaze as sharp as two razors.

"Slocum," Jess said, "is what I would call a town tamer. He's left a trail through Western towns from the Mississippi River to the Pacific shore. He's wanted for murder back in Georgia. I heard about him up in Socorro and even in Montana when I sold a herd of cattle up in Bozeman."

"Gosh," Hutch said, "what in hell is he doin' here in the valley?"

"That's what I'd like to know," Jess said. "And what was he doin' with Caleb Butterbean? Was Caleb carryin' anything with him on that sorry mule of his?"

"Nah, just them bags of pinyon nuts. They was full."

"So, he was down on Cactus Flat, where you men burned Lonnie to a crisp," Jess said.

"Likely," Cory said. "I never thought about that."

"So he either met Slocum down on the flat, or maybe met him down in Jackrabbit Valley."

"What's the difference?" Cory Windom asked.

Jess fixed him with a look of both contempt and pity.

"If they met down on Cactus Flat, it was likely they both saw what you did with Lonnie Taylor, you dumb bastard."

Cory winced. "Butterbean's always sneakin' around down there pickin' up pinyon nuts but we never saw him."

"How about Slocum?" Jess asked.

"No, sir, we never saw him until he come ridin' into town with Butterbean."

"They come in from the direction of the Ettinger mine, so they probably come from either Jackrabbit or Cactus Flat," Hutch said.

"A damned town tamer," Cordwainer muttered.

Then he looked at the three men. His gaze fell on each face in turn as his mind captured thoughts, worked them over, and formulated them into the words he was about to speak.

"Well, that makes it simple, then," Jess aid. "You men know what you have to do."

"What's that?" Creek asked.

"Bushwhack Slocum any way you can. I want his damned lamp put out. Pronto."

"Well, we know where he's stayin'," Hutch said. "We can pump a couple of barrels full of buckshot through his winder and splatter him all over that hotel room."

"Be easy," Creek said.

"Don't kid yourself, Joe," Jess said. "Slocum hasn't lived this long because he's a fool. Wherever you take him down, you'd better make sure he don't get up. I've heard stories about this bastard that would curl your hair. He won't be easy."

"We bushwhacked before, Jess," Cory said. "That prospector Jed Crane who wouldn't pay up, and Doolin, that Mick what insulted you one night at the Hoot Owl. Neither of them knew what hit 'em."

"And neither will Slocum," Joe said. The men had removed their hats when they sat down on the sofa and

Joe twirled his in his nervous fingers. Cory looked at the walls of the front room. They bore no pictures, but instead, rifles and carbines were on wooden pegs and over the hearth. A Kentucky rifle with a curly maple stock hung with a cow powder horn and a brass powder flask. It was a beautiful rifle made in Lancaster, Pennsylvania, in the 1830s by a master gunsmith. He had never been inside Jess's cabin before, and he was awestruck by all the pistols and knives dangling from wooden pegs and the long guns on display. He even saw a single-shot Remington shotgun leaning in one corner, as shiny as when it was brand new.

"While you're at it, boys," Jess said, "you might as well take care of Butterbean."

"Old Caleb?" Joe said in shocked surprise. "Why, he never hurt a flea and he ain't no count."

"If he saw you burn Taylor," Jess said, "he's got eyes and a mouth. You don't want no witnesses just in case he opens his trap at the Hoot Owl and names you boys as the ones he saw puttin' Taylor in the furnace."

"He's right," Hutch said. "Caleb might have seen us."

Cordwainer smiled.

"He probably did see you," Jess said. "Now get to it. I'll be in town tonight and I don't want to see either Slocum or Butterbean."

"That's mighty quick, boss," Cory said.

"Quick is better than slow," Cordwainer said. "Get it done."

The men stood up and put on their hats. They all looked sheepish as they raised hands to gesture goodbye to Cordwainer.

"See you at the Hoot Owl," Cordwainer said.

Cory was the last to go through the door. He turned and spoke to Jess.

"Better make it late, Jess. It might take a while."

"Two easy targets, Cory. Three against two."

Cory said nothing. He closed the door behind him.

Cordwainer picked up a pipe, filled the bowl with tobacco. He stood by the window and lit it as he watched the three men ride past the boulders and disappear. A man came around the side of the house and looked inside the window. He carried a Winchester that rested on one shoulder, his hand on the stock and lever.

Jess gestured for the man to come inside, then opened the door for him.

"Everything all right, Jess?" the man said.

"Maybe. You saw Hutch, Cory, and Joe ride out of here?"

"Sure. I was right outside in case you had need of me."

The man was Terry Bowker, and Jess trusted him.

"I want you to get Pat and Lou out here early this evening. Can you do that for me, Terry?"

"Sure, Jess. Bud's due to relieve me at four o'clock this afternoon. Pat and Lou are camped on the far end of Union Flat where I bunk. That soon enough?"

"Yeah. Make sure they get here before sundown."

"You got it, Jess. What's up?"

"I need them to take care of a little insurance matter. With those three who just left."

"An insurance matter?"

Terry was a small man, wiry and lean, with reddish hair, hazel eyes, wattles on his neck from a close call with a hanging tree when he was just a kid. Jess had saved him and hired him as a personal bodyguard.

"Let's just say I want Lou and Pat to track some trackers. Just in case."

"I got you, Jess." Terry chuckled. "Insurance."

"Who did you say was relieving you?" Jess asked.

"Bud Rafferty. He's like an owl at night. I swear he can see in the dark."

Jess laughed. "What I need is someone who can see in the daylight and not be spotted."

"You know what's best, Jess. Them are three good men, though. Whatever you got them to do for you, they'll likely do it."

Jess said nothing.

They were all stupid to his mind. Dumber than a sack full of metal washers.

But he didn't need smart at this point. He just needed sneaky, and those men fit the bill. They were experienced bushwhackers.

Just what he needed right now.

He puffed on his pipe and waved Terry back outside. He was hungry and it was just past noon. He hoped he would hear some good news by evening when he met Ruby and took her to the Hoot Owl. There he would pick up on the latest gossip, news of gold strikes, or fresh claims.

It was all part of his grand scheme and he wasn't going to let a man like Slocum spoil any of it, much less that dolt, Caleb Butterbean.

8

Slocum left Abby at The Excelsior while he rode Taylor's horse back to the Polygon House. He wrapped the reins around the hitch rail and walked back to his hotel.

"Miss Abby left a message for you, Mr. Slocum," Sammy said when Slocum stopped at the desk to pick up his key. "I'll be going off duty at four o'clock, when the night man, Donald Fenway, will take over the shift."

Sammy handed Slocum the key to Room 6.

"Thanks, Sammy. I'll be at lunch if anybody stops by."

"Yes, the dining room is open, sir."

"Food good?" Slocum said.

"Yes, sir, the food here is excellent."

"We'll see," Slocum said. "I could eat the southbound end of a northbound buffalo right now."

Sammy laughed, and Slocum walked into the dining room. There were a few diners, but he did not see the elderly people who were trying to find Lonnie Taylor. He wondered if they knew by now that Lonnie was dead. For that matter, he wondered if anyone in town knew, besides Caleb and Abby, and the men who'd murdered him.

He sat down at a table and ordered beefsteak, boiled potatoes, coleslaw, and peaches with cream. He ate slowly and smoked half of a cheroot before he went to his room. He placed his bedroll, saddlebags, and rifle on the floor and napped. When he awoke, the sun was setting in the west, and he looked out at the long shadows of the livery and the trees with dark puddles around their trunks.

Abby had said she would have him to supper in her suite around seven that evening, so he poured water from the pitcher in the bowl and dug out his razor, mug, and soap from his saddlebags. He shaved with cold water and changed his shirt. He smoked another cheroot and lit the lamp on the little table next to his bed.

Then, as he looked out the window, he arranged the two pillows under the blanket and cover on the bed so that anyone looking through his window would think that he was sleeping. He closed the window, but left the curtains open. He shoved his rifle, saddlebags, and bedroll under the bed and waited as the sky outside darkened and pools of light from the upstairs room left geometric designs on the ground behind the hotel, all yellow and golden as the twilight retreated into the dark maw of night.

The knock on the door brought Slocum to his feet. He had been sitting in a dark corner of the room looking out the window, listening for any sound outside. He opened the door.

"Mr. Slocum," the man in the doorway said, "I'm Donald Fenway, the night clerk. Miss Abby wishes me to bring you up to her suite."

Fenway was a dapper man in his mid-fifties, with a handlebar mustache, neatly trimmed pork-chop sideburns, slicked-down black hair parted in the middle, and close-set dark eyes that flanked a nose sporting a large pink wart on its tip. He wore pin-striped trousers, a white shirt, and suspenders that were a dusky green.

Slocum brushed his hair on both sides with the palms of his hands and stepped into the hall. He locked the door and slipped the key into his pocket. He squared his hat on his head and followed Fenway down the hall and up the stairs to the second floor.

He waited while the clerk knocked discreetly on the door. The door had no number on it. He heard the latch click and the door opened.

"Thank you, Don," Abby said to Fenway. "Please tell Steven to bring up our supper in fifteen minutes."

"I'll do that, Miss Abby. Good evening."

With that, Fenway was gone and Abby pulled Slocum into the room. The lamps were turned down low and there were dark shadows lazing on the carpets like silhouetted animals. The furnishings were not overly plush, but they showed good taste. Abby took his hat and hung it on a tree in the short hallway.

"You look very handsome tonight, Johnnie," she said as she took his hand and led him to an embroidered couch with two end tables and a coffee table. He saw a small bar against the wall.

"Must be the low light in here," he said.

Abby laughed.

"Our supper will be up soon. I know you want to go to the Hoot Owl tonight and meet with Caleb. I've got Kentucky bourbon. I know it's your favorite. As for me, I'm going to sip a little green crème de menthe. You can smoke if you like."

"Nice room," he said as he sat down and sank into the rose-patterned cushion.

"It's just for show," she said as she walked over to the bar and stood behind it, looking at him. "Wally stays here when he's in town and I entertain people who come up from Grizzly Lake to try and sell me hotel supplies or insurance policies."

Slocum saw ashtrays on both end tables. There were none on the low coffee table. He watched as Abby poured whiskey into a tumbler and then poured crème de menthe into a small snifter.

She carried the drinks over to the couch and set them on the coffee table. As she sat down beside him, he could smell her perfume. The lamplight made her soft hair shine, and the twin ringlets dangling in front of her ears sparkled. She wore a summery dress of gingham with a lace collar that was cut low enough so that he could see her bosom as it swelled against the green and white stripes of her bodice. Her pleated skirt was cream-colored with tiny bluebirds on pale blue patches of sky sewn into the fabric.

She patted Slocum's knee and smiled at him as she picked up her snifter.

"Tomorrow, I'll take you to see Wally," she said. "He's anxious to show you his mine and tell you about all the trouble he's had from Cordwainer."

Slocum picked up his whiskey glass and clinked it against Abby's snifter.

"I'm real anxious to see Wally, too," he said. He drank, holding the whiskey in his mouth for a few seconds before he swallowed it. He savored the warmth of the whiskey, the tangy smell that filled his nostrils. "I gather Cordwainer is trying to steal his claim, but can't find it."

"That's right," she said. "Wally took great care in filing. and no matter how many men Cordwainer sends to find out its location, Wally has managed to keep anyone from discovering where it is. It's a rich claim, I think."

"Is this what Cordwainer does?" Slocum asked. "Jump claims?"

"Yes, only he wouldn't call it that. He befriends prospectors and miners, stakes them sometimes, and if they find color, he moves in and takes over. There are a lot of prospectors who have disappeared after bringing gold dust and nuggets into town and meeting up with Cordwainer."

Slocum sipped from his glass again and looked around. There was a door at the far end of the modestly furnished room, and besides the bar, couch, and small tables, the walls were decorated only with some Currier & Ives prints and a tintype of Halcyon Valley just after the first gold rush there some dozen or so years before.

"I have three rooms here," she said. "This is what I call my parlor. The sitting room is in the center, where I have a table set for supper, and the last room is the bedroom, or if you want to be fancy, the boudoir."

They both laughed and their eyes met in an exchange of intimate meanings beyond her words.

Abby seemed worldly enough, Slocum thought, but he still thought of her as a little girl in pigtails with freckles dotting her cheeks and nose. Now, of course, she was grown and the freckles were gone.

"Johnnie, before we have supper, there's something I want to ask you."

"Sure," he said.

She sipped from her snifter as if drawing courage from the alcohol.

"Maybe I'm being too forward," she said, her voice dropping into a lower register, "but I was wondering if, when you get back from the Hoot Owl, you might want to come up here for a little nightcap."

"Abby, you don't have to ask such a question. I'd be mighty happy to have a brandy with you when I come back to the hotel."

She grabbed one of his hands and squeezed it.

"I want to give you more than brandy," she said. "If you'll come up here after you talk to Caleb."

He sensed that, at heart, Abby was a lonely woman. She was conducting business with her brother, but from what he'd seen so far, there were not many eligible suitors in Halcyon Valley. And if Cordwainer had his eye on her, that put her off the market as far as attracting local men to her doorstep.

"I'm at your disposal, dear Abby," he said with a gentleness in his voice that made Abby shudder as she looked deep into his eyes.

"Ever since I was a little girl," she said, "I've thought about you. Oh, at first it was like an uncle, then a father after ours died, but then . . . over the years, as I grew, I thought of you differently."

They both jumped when they heard the knock on the door.

"Oh, dear," she said. "Steve's here with our supper already."

"We can finish this talk over supper," he said, and rose with her as she left the couch to open the door.

He watched her walk across the room, and the flash of her pretty young legs caused his heart to quicken, and he admired the bounce of her buttocks, the trim thighs outlined beneath her skirt.

She opened the door and there was the man named

Steve with a small cart covered with a white tablecloth. Tendrils of steam crept through the fabric and the smell of meat and cooked veal filled the room.

Abby walked to the far door and opened it. Steve wheeled the cart inside. Abby turned and beckoned to Slocum.

She had a smile on her face that melted something inside him.

The way her fingers moved and that look in her eyes meant that she was inviting him to something a lot more important than supper.

The waiting was going to be hard, he thought as he strode across the room, his stovepipe boots barely making a sound on the deep pile carpet.

Yes, he thought, it was going to be hard as hell to wait for that nightcap.

9

Slocum saw the small dining table with its white table-cloth. The waiter, Steve Cooley, removed the cloth over the cart and began setting warm plates, covered dishes, wineglasses, and wine on the table. There was a single tall candle burning in a brass holder in the center of the table and neatly folded napkins beneath the silverware.

"Will that be all, Miss Abby?" Steve asked as he finished setting the food on the table.

"Yes, Steve," she said. "Thanks. If I need anything, I'll ring the bell downstairs."

"Yes, ma'am," he said. He nodded to Slocum as he passed with the empty cart and went out the front door.

"I'll lock the door so we won't be disturbed," she said, and walked to the front door. She returned in a few seconds and closed the door to the dining salon behind her.

"Please sit down, Johnnie," she said, and waved him to a comfortable chair with embroidered padding.

Slocum sat down. He could smell the food, and his stomach issued a low growl. Abby sat down and began removing the metal covers over the main dishes.

"I hope you like veal cutlets," she said. "And there is asparagus and new potatoes, hot biscuits and butter. Will you pour the wine?"

Slocum picked up one of the bottles. It bore a label that proclaimed it to be Cabernet Sauvignon and it was from Bordeaux, France. All he had to do was pull the cork. The wax had been broken and the cork pulled up slightly on both bottles. The wine had an aroma of Gallic vineyards and musty cellars. He poured both glasses half full as Abby dished up each plate with a fancy silver spatula.

"It's all beautiful," Slocum said.

She handed him his plate and picked up her glass.

"Here's to you, Johnnie," she said, toasting him, "with thanks from Wally and me for coming, and the wish that your visit will be pleasant and memorable."

"So far," he said, "it's both a pleasure and something I'll never forget. You look lovely tonight, Abby, and you set a fine table."

She laughed.

"Steve deserves all the credit for that," she said.

They clinked their glasses together and sipped the wine. Slocum felt the warmth of her across the table and noticed how dainty she was as they both cut up the veal and ate slowly. They talked of old times and there was no mention of Wally's situation or Cordwainer.

Abby slipped off her shoes and tickled Slocum's knees under the table. She gave him a coy smile. He reached down and touched her foot, began to massage each toe as if she were a child. He smiled at her and she drank a sip of wine.

Somehow, they managed to eat their supper, but it was plain to both of them that there would be a lingering dessert after the table was cleared away.

After supper, Abby pulled a dangling cord by a window, and after Steve had cleared away their supper dishes, she ushered Slocum back into the front room. To his surprise, she went behind the bar and returned with a bottle of *aguardiente* and a box of cheroots.

"Wally bought these for your visit," she said. "The brandy is from *Bodegas de Santo Tomas* in Ensenada, Mexico, and the cheroots he had sent to him from New Orleans a month ago."

Slocum opened the box, which turned out to be a humidor with a red cedar lining. The aroma was powerful. She lit his cigar for him and poured brandy for them both.

She sat next to him on the divan and sniffed the smoke as she sipped from her small snifter.

"My, that's good," she said.

"It's all good, Abby," Slocum said as he clinked her glass with his. "And I've made a decision."

Her eyes danced with surprise as the lamplight struck her raised head.

"Pray tell," she teased, "whatever are you talking about?"

"I'm not going to the Hoot Owl tonight. The brandy and the company are too fine to waste. I'll see Caleb another day."

Abby exploded in glee.

She set her glass down on the coffee table and clapped her hands.

"Oh, Johnnie," she exclaimed, "I couldn't be happier. I want to take your boots off and just look at you enjoying your cigar. And the brandy, of course."

"And you," he said, a slight husk in his voice.

"Yes, yes," she said, and slid closer to him until their hips were touching.

When Slocum had finished his cigar and the snifters were empty, Abby grabbed Slocum's arm and drew him close to her.

"Would you like to see my bedroom?" she said.

"Now?"

"Yes, now," she whispered into his ear and squeezed his arm. She kissed him on the cheek and then stood up. She took his hand in hers and pulled him to his feet.

It was all he could do to resist taking her into his arms and kissing those enticing lips. He felt a tug at his trousers as his cock unfolded and began to harden.

The bedroom was small and neat. It was neither a man's nor a woman's in its spare furnishings, its plain brown drapery, the night tables, the hurricane lamp on the dresser. But it smelled of the fresh lilacs arranged in a vase on one of the end tables.

Abby lit a small lamp on one of the tables. The light bathed the lower edges of the bed with an amber mist while the comforter and pillows were shrouded in near darkness. There was a wardrobe standing against one wall, and a chair and footstool that were out of the way, but convenient.

"Does this suit you, Johnnie?" she murmured as she sat demurely on the bed, spreading her arms wide.

"Abby, you make any room you're in more than suitable. Don't you know that?"

"I'm not used to such compliments," she said.

He walked over to her and took her face in his hands. He looked into her eyes for a long moment, then bent down to kiss her appealing lips.

She opened her mouth slowly and he could taste the

brandy. But he also could smell her womanly musk, the heady aroma of her sex. She was not only willing, he decided, but eager.

"I want you, Johnnie," she breathed when he broke the kiss and took his hands away.

"I want you, too, Abby," he said.

"I've wanted you for a long time," she said. "Secretly, of course."

"Maybe I was just waiting for you to grow up and become a woman," he said, his voice gravelly with desire.

"Well, here I am. A woman grown."

"It's time, then," he said, and she reached out with one hand and touched the bulge in his pants. He winced with the thrill of her touch.

"Yes," she said, her voice low and alluring, "it's time. I want that. I want you to cover me and hold me."

He stepped away and she pulled down the covers and exposed the white linen sheets. She began to unbutton her blouse. Slocum walked over to the chair and began to strip as he watched her slip out of her skirt and pull her panties down. Then, she stood naked next to the bed as he unbuckled his gun belt and wrapped his pistol and holster into a bundle and set them on the footstool. He took off his stovepipe boots and pulled his trousers off, laid them over the back of the chair. Then he removed his shirt and shorts and plopped them onto the chair. He walked to her naked, and took her in his arms.

They kissed and she felt his manhood rise and touch the folds of her cunt as if it were seeking that nest between her legs. She shivered and he held her tight against him. Her breasts mashed against his wide chest and they were soft and yielding, the nipples turning hard as she rubbed her breast against his.

He pushed her gently down on the bed and they lay side by side, gazing into each other's eyes. He touched the nipples on her breasts and kissed the nubbins until she squirmed with a growing lust. Then he kissed both breasts and pulled on the taut nipples with his mouth, his teeth gently grazing the rough edges that had hardened to acorn-like kernels.

His left hand touched her tummy and slid down into her thatch, caressing the wiry hairs that hid the cleft. Her body undulated and he slid a finger into her cunt and probed until he found the clitoris. She jumped with a sudden spasm as he stroked the tiny organ that brought such great pleasure to a woman when aroused.

"Oh, yes, Johnnie," she sighed. "This is what I've been waiting for."

"There is more," he gruffed as he slipped atop her and covered her small body with his.

They kissed and he ran his tongue inside her mouth. When he withdrew, she slipped her tongue into his mouth and panted like a hungry kitten as he poked his cock against the portals of her cunt, sliding the mushroomed head up and down until she spread her legs even wider and grabbed his back with both hands. He felt the tips of her fingernails digging into his flesh.

She reached down and grabbed his shaft and guided it into her steaming pussy, her body rising to take him inside her, her hips arcing over the bed as he pushed and thrust his manhood into the steaming cauldron of her sex.

"Oh, yes," she exclaimed. "That's it. That's heaven."

She was not a virgin, but she was not very experienced either, Slocum thought. There was no hymen to break, but she was small and tight and her pussy began to squeeze his cock as if it had fingers. He drove in deeper and her body arched. He felt her body jolt with pleasure as she bucked with her first orgasm.

Her scream was soft in his ears, like the cry of an animal.

He stroked her, in and out, long and deep, and their bodies began to rise and fall in the ancient rhythm of lovemaking as if they were erotic dancers on a dark stage.

There was pleasure in her loins and the little girl in her disappeared and was transformed into the body and mystery of a full grown woman in season.

She gushed with warm fluids and drenched his cock with the oils of her passion.

Abby bucked beneath him with orgasm after orgasm. And each one seemed more tumultuous than the one before. Slocum had to use all of his mental agility to stave off his own spurts of pleasure. He wanted to take her to the heights and let her float there in that cloud of pure wonder for as long as he could.

Both of them were slick with sweat, and their twin musks melded into a heady scent that was more erotic than the most expensive perfume.

She gripped him tightly against her, and he slid to the very core of her womb and filled her until the veins on his organ were engorged with blood and his size had expanded to enormous proportions.

The night hovered outside the window, filled with moon and starlight that gave the drapes a luminosity shimmering to the tempo of the shaking bed, where the two lovers thrashed and entwined their bodies into a single embrace that blotted out all but the highest sensations of the heart and spirit.

10

Caleb Butterbean felt the thin hairs on the back of his neck prickle as he sat at one end of the long bar at the Hoot Owl Saloon. He was facing the door so that he could spot Slocum when he came in. He had a can of roasted pinyon nuts on the bartop and a mug of warm beer next to it.

He turned his head to look out over the tables where men were drinking and playing cards.

Someone was staring at him.

When Caleb spotted the man, he turned quickly away and bowed his head slightly to say something to the man standing next to him.

Hutch had been the man who had stared at Caleb and the man Hutch was talking to now was Joe Creek.

They were two of the men who had murdered Lonnie Taylor, burned him to death.

Caleb felt a queasy feeling in his stomach.

Did they know he had seen them down on Cactus

Flat that morning? He had been quiet and kept himself hidden, but there was no telling. They might have seen him or his mule when they rode off. And they probably saw him and Slocum ride into town and had put two and two together.

And where in hell was John Slocum?

Hutch turned to meet two men who came up to him. Caleb recognized them as gunslingers who worked for Cordwainer—Pat Morris and Lou Jessup. They both had reputations as killers and the gossip in town was that they had spent years in a Southern penitentiary. All Caleb knew was that they never did any honest work and they always had money to spend.

He saw them talking to Hutch and Joe Creek, but not loud enough for their voices to carry. Hutch kept nodding as Pat whispered into his ear and then an odd expression transformed his facial features. His look went from blank to a scowl and then to a snarling countenance. His eyes narrowed. Joe Creek got up and grabbed Hutch's arm. Joe pulled Hutch away from the two other men and they walked quickly across the room, wending their way between tables and staring straight ahead. In moments they were out the door.

Lou and Pat stayed where they had been. Both looked in Caleb's direction, but their faces were impassive. They ordered drinks from one of the scantily clad glitter gals and sat down. Pat kept looking at him every now and then, but Lou did not glance his way.

Caleb stared at the batwing doors of the saloon but nobody came in. He began to feel very uncomfortable when he noticed that Pat was still glancing at him every few minutes.

He finished his beer and decided not to order another.

"Leavin' so soon, Caleb?" the bartender said as

Caleb pushed his empty glass across the bar, picked up his lard can of pinyon nuts, and got off the barstool.

"Yeah, Harry."

"Was you waitin' for someone?"

"Sort of," Caleb said as he tucked the can under his left arm.

"'Night Caleb," Harry said as he lifted the empty glass with its streaks of foam and amber residue.

Caleb walked briskly out of the saloon and into the night. He strode along the hitch rail to his mule and put the can of nuts in his saddlebag. He unwrapped the reins and climbed onto the mule's back.

He rode toward the hanging tree, its bare arms scratching the starry sky. Now every shape in the shadows was menacing. It was as if he had a premonition that something bad was going to happen. As he rode past the tree, toward his own digs, he looked back toward the saloon.

No one was following him.

He began to relax and wondered if he should go into town and stop in at The Excelsior and ask about Slocum. No, he decided. It had been a long day. He was tired and wanted to do some panning the next day, perhaps in the creek or the pond, where there was always some color to be found. He didn't need money right away, and if he found ten dollars' worth of dust clinging to the black dolomite in his pan, he would be satisfied with that day's work.

He heard the faint whicker of a horse and it seemed to Caleb that his blood jumped from his heart and shot into every nerve along his spine.

"Who's there?" he called in a quavery voice.

There was no answer.

Had he imagined it? He turned his head and listened,

but heard nothing more. He was well past the hanging tree and turned on the dim road to his cabin.

That was when he saw a shadow move. No, he saw two shadows detach from the deeper shadows of the pines just ahead of him.

Caleb's heart jumped in his chest and throbbed in his eardrums. He pulled on the reins to turn his mule away from the menacing shadows.

"Hold on there, Caleb," called a voice.

He halted the mule. The voice sounded familiar.

"Who are ye?" he said.

Hutch stepped toward him. Beside him was Joe Creek. Both men carried scatterguns. He saw the moonlight glint off the twin barrels of both weapons.

"I'm the Reaper, Caleb," Hutch said in a casual, disarming tone of voice.

"Huh?"

"The Grim Reaper," Creek said, and both he and Hutch laughed.

They walked closer and Caleb heard two unmistakable metallic sounds. Then he heard two more as both approaching men pulled the hammers back on their shotguns.

"I got no quarrel with either of you two fellers," Caleb said, his voice reduced to a thin squeak. "Just leave me be."

But he knew it was too late to stop what was surely coming.

Hutch and Creek were close. They raised their shotguns to their shoulders and took aim.

Caleb kicked the mule in the flanks and ducked.

Both shotguns exploded and belched orange fire, smoke, and heavy lead pellets.

As the first balls struck him, Caleb felt a dozen pains, as if he had been attacked by hornets. Then there were two more explosions, and more double-ought buckshot ripped into his body. The mule's forelegs crumpled and it fell to its side, mortally wounded.

Caleb gasped for air, but blood in his throat blocked the passage. He wheezed and vomited blood as he struck the ground.

He saw the stars spin in the dark sky and his mouth filled with blood. The agony drifted away as his brain shut down and the darkness dropped on him like a leaden sash weight.

Hutch and Creek reloaded their shotguns and stepped over the mule's neck to look down at Caleb. Dark blood made a half-dozen puddles in the road. Caleb's heart was no longer pumping and he was not breathing.

"No need to waste another shot shell on this piece of meat," Creek said.

"Nope. Old Caleb's as dead as dead can be."

"And his blamed mule, too. You done blowed one of its eyes clean out, Hutch."

"Let's get the hell out of here, Joe, before we draw a crowd."

"Yeah. We got one more to go, Hutch. I hope Lou and Pat know we done our job."

"Part of it anyway," Hutch said.

"The next part should be real easy."

"Yeah, it should," Hutch said.

The two men returned to where their horses were tied and mounted up. They shoved their shotguns into scabbards and rode toward town, past the hanging tree and over the flat, avoiding any of the roads.

They rode up slowly behind The Excelsior Hotel and

dismounted some fifty yards away from the back entrance. They pulled their shotguns from their sheaths and stalked toward the rear of the hotel.

As they approached, Hutch looked at the window to Slocum's room.

He held out a hand and stopped Creek from taking his next step.

"Bastard even left a light on for us," he whispered to Creek. "That's his room."

Creek looked and saw the pale orange glow of a lamp shining like mist outside a window on the first floor.

"Mighty nice of him," he breathed.

The two men went through the rail fence and into the hotel compound. They crept up to the window. Creek stood on tiptoe and looked into the room.

Hutch did the same.

They both saw the bed with its lumps under the coverlet.

Both nodded to each other and ducked back down beneath the windowsill.

They squeezed the triggers of their shotguns slowly and partially as they pulled four hammers back.

"On three," Hutch said.

Creek nodded.

Hutch counted.

"One, two, three."

Both men stood up and poked their shotguns at the bed, their barrels touching the glass. They pulled the triggers. Hammers fell. Percussion caps exploded. Both guns spewed fire and buckshot through the window, shattering the glass. The bedding jumped as it was ripped by dozens of lead pellets. Some of the wood splintered on the wall and bed.

Both men ran toward the fence, satisfied that they had done their job.

They mounted their horses and put distance between them and the hotel. They rode to the Polygon House and hitched their horses to the rail.

"I ain't tired," Joe said.

"Me neither."

"Let it quiet down some and we'll go on back to the Hoot Owl."

"Yeah, Jess ought to be there by now. He'll want to know he don't have to worry none over Butterbean or Slocum."

The two men waited a good fifteen minutes. They rolled quirlies and smoked.

When they were finished, they rode down a back street toward the Hoot Owl.

"That's what I like about Halcyon Valley," Hutch said.

"What's that?" Joe asked.

"It's a right quiet place."

Both men laughed. They ejected the empty shot shells and reloaded, stuffing the empty hulls in their pockets.

There was a bunch of people outside the saloon when they rode up.

"What's up?" Creek asked one of those standing outside.

"Somebody got shot up past the hangin' tree," a man said.

"Who?" Hutch asked.

The man shrugged.

"Hell if I know. Probably some prospector who couldn't hold his likker."

Hutch and Creek dismounted and walked inside the saloon. They spotted Cordwainer. He was talking to the constable, Herb Mayfair. Herb looked ashen and half drunk.

When they approached their boss, Cordwainer looked at them and smiled.

It was, Hutch thought, just like a pat on the back.

11

As the moon rose over the mountains, it beamed into the window of Abby's room. It seemed to dust the drapes with a pewter sheen and they glowed like the gowns of fashion mannequins in a darkened store window. The room breathed and panted with the voices of the two lovers on the bed. They made love slowly, with Slocum pumping in and out of Abby's wet and steamy sheath in long smooth strokes.

"So nice," she breathed. "So, so good." She drawled the words in a languid sighing voice that seemed to match his rhythm.

His hands gripped her thighs and he pulled upward on them as he dipped downward, the pleasure in him radiating from his swollen organ through every fiber of his body as if there was some electrical connection between them, a force that could not be calculated or measured, but was all pervasive, like the universe itself.

"So good," he repeated as the seconds slowed to

nearly a standstill in that moment when he reached the very mouth of her womb and her body trembled and quivered like some skewered creature caught in a trap.

What is this wonder? he asked himself. What is this force between a man and a woman that blots out all reason and just whips the senses into a frenzy like wild horses galloping over a hill in some unknown region of earth? How can a pigtailed girl grow into a voluptuous woman and compress time so that the leap goes unnoticed and the change seems so abrupt? How is it that she and I are here in this magical darkness when all the world is in some kind of mindless stupor? This, he thought, is life, the very essence of life, and nothing matters but our arms stretching toward heaven to touch the hands of a god for one fleeting, but imperishable moment.

"Johnnie," she cooed, and her voice jarred him from his fleeting reveries even as the pleasure of their coupling seeped through him like warm wine.

"Something wrong?" he asked.

"No," she said, her voice soft and silken as a summer rain on sodden leaves. "I want to get on top. Please."

"Sure," he said.

"I want to feel more of you, make you touch different places inside me."

He rolled from atop her and lay on his back. She climbed over him and grasped his cock as she lifted her hips. She held him fast as she descended, sheathing his cock inside the folds of her sex as if it were an oiled dagger.

"Ah, ah," she breathed, and rose and fell while two of her fingers clasped the base of his prick as if to hold his shaft in place. Slocum lay there, letting Abby take command, letting her find more pleasure from her dominant position. And she nearly swooned as she shuddered with still another orgasm when he was deep within her. She cried out and the cries were full of joy and pleasure, almost exultant, as if she had discovered some hidden treasure.

Sweat oiled her neck and breasts. She looked like a mermaid emerging from the sea as she dipped her lithe body up and down in a slow rhythmic motion that was like some physical exercise to tone the body. She was light as a feather, Slocum thought, yet the warm wetness of her pussy was like balm to his exploding senses.

Lightning flashed in his brain. Volcanoes erupted and the earth of the bed shook with temblors as she climaxed again and again, each time more savage and feral than the last. She might have been screaming, he thought, but she was holding it in so that only he could hear the exclamations of her pleasure. And the sound of her voice was thrilling, brought him to a heightened excitement so powerful he had to concentrate on the ceiling's impersonal drabness to keep from spilling his seed inside her.

Finally, Abby collapsed atop him and he held her in his arms. He was still inside her, but she was exhausted, her body sleek with perspiration.

"Enough?" he whispered as he stroked her hair. Her head was lying on his chest and she felt so small and vulnerable.

"More," she said. "But you have to do it, Johnnie."

Then she lifted herself from his anchor and rolled onto her back.

He rubbed her flat and slick tummy and slowly rose above her once again.

Abby spread her legs to receive him and lay there willing and wanton as a woman in season.

Slocum entered her, slid gently into that valley of luxuriant warmth, and stroked her slow and steady while her breathing subsided and became more regular.

"Oh," she said, "that's what I need, that feeling inside me, that slow sweet stroking that makes me feel warm and wanted all over. You're so good, Johnnie. I've never felt anything like this before."

He said nothing, but looked down at her face. It was a face suffused with rapture. Her mouth was partially open and her hair like a fan on the pillow, a study in beauty that would linger in his mind long after they uncoupled and fell back to earth.

She moaned and he increased his rhythm.

"Yes, yes," she said, her voice a crackling croak in her throat. "I want you to come. I want you to shoot your milk inside me until I scream."

"Sure?" he asked.

"Do it, Johnnie," she said in a clear voice. "Do it now."

He drove into her hard and fast and his rhythm increased until it was a crescendo that made them soar beyond the gravity of earth and sail even higher. She screamed and he shot seeds into her, the warm and milky essence of himself. He spurted and spurted as they both floated down from some incredible altitude.

"Ah, ah," she sighed, and wriggled her hips back and forth. She squeezed him until there was no more spurting, no more seed to issue from his loins.

"El poco muerte," he said. "The little death, the Spanish call it."

"It's not like death," she said. "It's like being born in fire and ice."

"It only lasts a second, but it seems so eternal, Abby."

He went limp inside her and rolled from her sated

body. He was both drained of energy and filled with it. It felt as if he had been through a little death and then reborn, resurrected in a twinkling by some mystical force beyond all comprehension.

"The little death," she mused, her eyelashes fluttering as she blinked in search of words to describe her complex and tangled feelings. "Yes, I can see that, in some mysterious way."

She reached out a hand and he took it and kissed it.

"Thank you, Johnnie," she said. "You made me so happy. Happier than I've ever been."

"You're some woman, Abby. My pleasure."

"Our pleasure," she said.

Just then, they heard four rapid explosions from downstairs and outside.

Slocum rose up.

"Shotguns," he said to himself.

Four blasts and the sound of glass shattering and wood splintering.

"Do you have a window that looks out over the back of the hotel?" he asked as he slid out of bed.

"No, my rooms are in front. What's going on, Johnnie?"

"I don't know, but those were shotguns going off, two of them."

She sat up and her eyes rolled wildly in their sockets.

"What could it be?"

"I'm damned sure going to find out," he said. "You stay here."

"Will you be back?" she asked.

"Unless I run into something that I can't get out of," he said.

He dressed quickly, strapped on his gun belt, and left through the door. Abby stood there, watching him.

"Lock it," he said.

She nodded numbly and then closed the door behind him.

Slocum took the stairs two steps at a time and reached the lobby.

The night clerk was standing in the center of the lobby, a bewildered look on his face.

"What's going on?" Donald Fenway asked when he saw Slocum.

"Didn't you hear those shots?"

"Yes, yes, I heard them. I think they came from . . ."

Slocum didn't let him finish. He dashed down the hall to his room.

He did not go in, but he could smell the burnt powder seeping from under the door, the acrid smell of cordite.

He ducked low and pushed open the back door. He stopped in the shadows and listened. Far off, he heard the faint sound of hoofbeats.

Then he walked to his window and saw the shattered glass. Shards lay on the ground and white smoke hung in the air like shimmering gauze in the white glare of the moonlight.

He looked at the ground around the window. The men, at least two of them, he reasoned, had not ejected their shot shells. They had just run off like cowards. They probably thought that he was dead, blasted to pieces by four shotgun blasts.

He went back inside the hotel and put the key in his lock. He opened the door. The lamp was still burning. The room stank of black powder and there were wisps of smoke hanging like cobwebs above his bed.

He walked over and looked down at his bedding. The floor was strewn with feathers and striped fabric, the covers shredded into rags. He picked up one of the lead balls.

"Double-ought buck," he said to himself.

The side of the bed was pocked with raw holes, and splinters lay like broken matchsticks on the floor.

If he had been sleeping in that bed, he would be dead, stone dead.

Slocum took one last look at the tattered remnants of his bed. He walked over to the lamp and turned down the wick until it went out.

He retrieved his rifle, saddlebags, and bedroll from under his bed and walked out of the room. He did not lock the door.

He knew where he was going to sleep that night.

And he was pretty sure he knew who had tried to murder him.

Somebody in town was running scared.

Come daylight, he vowed, he'd check those horse tracks and find out who the two bushwhackers were. One of them, he was sure, was the man they called Hutch.

Anger boiled in him as he thought about Lonnie Taylor and the way he had died.

Now they had come after him.

Big mistake, he thought.

This time, those killers had picked the wrong man.

And like the fools they were, they had missed. They had only killed a bed.

An empty one at that.

12

Slocum chased two men into a sun-ruddied canyon below monumental rock formations that identified the landscape as Arizona on a summer morn. Inside the towering walls of the canyon, the two men multiplied into a dozen, and before he reached the end, they had metamorphosed into a swarm of bees with gigantic stingers, furry bodies, and leather wings. He turned his horse, but it was too late. The bees came after him and smothered him, slashing his horse to ribbons and pushing hard on his chest.

He awoke, wide-eyed, to see the lovely features of Abby inches from his sleep-clogged eyes. She had a pillow in her hands and was pressing down on his chest.

He looked at the window. The drapes were pulled open and he saw twinkling stars fading against a pale blue horizon above the mountains. There was a rim of cream behind the peaks, and it rose and swallowed stars while the blue faded.

"Huh?" he said.

Abby laughed. "You said you wanted to get going before sunup," she said, tossing the pillow against the headboard. "Well, it's dawn and I've been up for hours."

"You have?" He sat up, ran fingers through his shock of unruly black hair.

"Yes," she said, "and I've been busy. I saw your room and I went to the livery and had Alvaro saddle your horse and leave it out in front of the hotel at the hitch rail."

"Thanks, Abby. I have to get cracking, then."

She jumped off the bed.

He saw that she was wearing a riding skirt, boots, and a chambray blouse.

"Do you want breakfast before you start tracking the men who shot into your room last night?"

He threw the covers aside and started to dress.

"No," he said. "I never eat before I go hunting."

"Johnnie, I know you want to get those men, but I want to take you to Wally's mine today."

"Once I find their tracks, that's all I need for now. I'll be back in a few minutes. Is your horse out front?"

"Yes," she said.

"I'll meet you there in a half hour or so."

Her face lit up as if a photographer had set off phosphorous in a tray.

He dressed quickly and strapped on his gun belt.

"We'll be gone all day?" he asked her.

"Most of it. We have to make sure none of Cordwainer's men follow us, and Wally wants to show you his mine and tell you what's at stake in Halcyon Valley."

"I'll lug my saddlebags and rifle down to my horse and tie on my bedroll. It has a sawed-off shotgun wrapped inside."

"I'll keep an eye on your horse. By the way, Alvaro told me his name, Ferro."

"Yeah," Slocum said. "It means 'iron' in Spanish. He's a long-distance horse, and sometimes I think he's made of iron."

"I'll walk downstairs with you," she said. "And, Johnnie . . ."

He turned at the door to look at her.

"Be careful," she said.

Fifteen minutes later, Slocum was in the alley behind the hotel. He crawled through the rail fence to his shattered window and studied the tracks that were now lit by the growing light from the sun.

He was careful to step on bare ground where there were no boot prints. He saw the fresher tracks of two men. One of the tracks matched the earlier ones that had aged or were obliterated by the newer tracks. This one he studied very carefully because he surmised it belonged to the man he had identified as Hutch.

Slocum was able to tell a great deal by studying those boot tracks. Hutch's right sole had a nick in the edge, a cut mark of some sort, and his left heel was rounded on one edge as if he favored that leg. It appeared that he was slightly bowlegged.

The other track revealed a man slightly lighter in weight than Hutch. His soles also bore distinctive marks. The toes of both boots appeared to be scuffed as if he had rubbed them on rocks or some metal material, such as a boot scraper. And both heels were starting to get round on the outside edges, suggesting that he was even more bowlegged than Hutch.

Slocum filed this information in his memory and retraced the steps the men had taken after firing off two shotguns. He saw that they ran to the rail fence, crawled through, and then ran some yards up the alley, where he encountered a maze of hoof marks.

With his practiced eye for tracking, Slocum could tell that the horses had been ground-tied in one spot. There were, as well, piles of horse dung scattered about, and places where the earth was pocked by streams of urine. He walked over slowly, bent down, and examined the maze, sorting out the tracks of both horses as they entered and exited the alley.

He saw which horse Hutch had mounted by the boot tracks spaced close together and then, when the man had mounted, the right footprint was smeared slightly as his left foot stepped into the stirrup. There was more pressure on the ball of the right foot just before he had lifted himself into the saddle.

Slocum studied the hoof marks of that horse, squatting down to look at a clear impression of first the left hind foot and then the other three. The iron shoes were showing signs of wear and these were distinctive.

One hoof had a worn heel on the outside, and another bore tiny grooves where the horse had probably scraped a rocky patch of ground, or pawed at a small stone to overturn it.

As for the other set of tracks, the shoes were worn, and one, the left hind shoe, dragged something along with it, perhaps a chunk of prickly pear cactus or a twig, so that it left a separate scraping track alongside the hoof. As for the other three hooves, they were worn at the heels and toes as if the rider had climbed some steep slopes often enough to wear down those portions of the shoe.

Again, Slocum committed what he had seen to memory. He walked back onto the street and headed for the front of the hotel. He saw Abby and her dun standing alongside Ferro.

"Ready?" he said.

"Yes. Did you find what you were looking for?"

"I could track those two men in my sleep," he said. "I could almost tell you how tall their horses are and what they had for supper."

Abby laughed.

"Do you know who shot at your room? How many were there?"

"Two men," he said. "I know the name of one of them."

"Oh? What's his name?"

"Hutch," he said.

"Al Hutchins," she said, and it seemed to Slocum that her eyes went cloudy for a second. "He works for Cordwainer."

"I suspect both men work for Cordwainer," he said.

"I'm sure you're right."

He unwrapped the reins from the hitch rail and started to step toward his left stirrup when Abby held up a hand to halt him. He stopped and looked at her as she rubbed the cheek of her horse.

"Johnnie," she said, "I just talked to Sammy, my day clerk. He was just coming on. He had some bad news."

"Oh?" Slocum's eyebrows arched.

"He said there was quite a commotion at the Hoot Owl last night. He could hear it from his cabin, so he walked over and saw a crowd outside."

Something prickled under Slocum's scalp as if someone had sprinkled black pepper in his hair.

"Well, what was going on?" Slocum asked, dreading Abby's reply.

"While he was there, a wagon pulled up and men all started talking at once. Some of them looked inside the bed and one or two of them vomited. So Sammy walked over to the wagon to see what was inside it. It made him sick, he said."

Slocum's mind raced and he thought of the night before. He was supposed to go to the Hoot Owl himself and meet a man.

"It was Caleb, wasn't it?" he said.

Abby jerked from the shock of the word.

"Yes, it was Caleb Butterbean," she said. "He was dead."

"Murdered?"

"Well, the constable was there, drunk as usual. And so was Jess Cordwainer and some of his men. When people asked what had happened, Herb Mayfair started shooing them all away. He told one of the men that Caleb had probably gone bird hunting and fallen off his mule and shot himself."

"Bird hunting at night?"

"That's what Sammy thought. From what he could tell, Caleb's body was riddled with buckshot. He had bloody holes in his face and neck, and his clothes were shredded and torn with holes. He thought Caleb had been shot more than once. There were just too many holes and too much blood."

"Damn," Slocum said. "I should have been there. If I had gone to the Hoot Owl, Caleb would still be alive."

"Or both of you would have died. Johnnie, these are ruthless men. That's why my brother sent for you. He can't fight them alone, and he can't hide from them much longer."

"Still, I blame myself. I should have met with Caleb. Maybe—"

"Stop talking that way, Johnnie," she said. "Come on. We've got a ways to ride and maybe we can avoid being followed this early in the day."

"All right."

"We can talk more about this along the way," she said.

"I'd like to see where Caleb was shot, study the tracks. Sometimes I can see things that an unpracticed eye would miss."

"Well, Sammy said that Caleb was killed at a fork in the road to his place. I can show you where it is. He said something else, too, which might help you find out who murdered poor Caleb."

"What's that?" Slocum asked.

"The men who shot Caleb killed his mule, too. It might still be there. Or if not, somebody may have dragged the animal off the road."

"If it's out there, I can look for buzzards circling in the sky," he said. "I ought to go out there right now."

"No, Johnnie, don't," she said. She pulled her reins over her horse's neck and climbed into the saddle. "You can do that after you and Wally have talked."

"I guess that dead mule will be there for a few days," he said.

He climbed into the saddle and they pulled away from the hotel. He was not surprised that Abby headed for the fringe of trees beyond the town flat. She kept looking back to see if they were being followed. Slocum started doing the same, but he couldn't get Caleb Butterbean out of his mind. One or two men had bushwhacked the poor old prospector in the dead of night. No man deserved to die like that. And certainly not Caleb.

There was only one explanation he could come up with when he thought about it.

Caleb had been slaughtered because the men who had burned Lonnie Taylor to a charred crisp down on Cactus Flat knew that Caleb had seen them. And that was probably why the same men were bent on killing Slocum. It was a dirty shame that Caleb had paid the price for being an innocent bystander, for seeing what he was not supposed to see.

Well, Slocum thought, those men may have put Caleb six feet under, but they would pay with their own lives sure as hell was hot.

As the surviving witness to the death of Lonnie Taylor, he was obligated to obtain justice for both men.

Such crimes should not go unpunished, he said to himself.

In the thin mountain air, his head was clear. He knew who he was going after, and if his hunch was right, there were more than two men involved in the murder of Caleb Butterbean.

And one of them was surely Jess Cordwainer.

13

Slocum rode alongside Abby through thick timber and terrain dotted with massive boulders and rocky outcroppings. They rode around deadfalls and down into shallow ravines, up small hills and across game trails. They saw deer and heard the plaintive pipings of mountain quail. Slocum realized that they were not following any marked trails or paths, but were deliberately sticking to hard ground and thick brush.

Although both looked over their shoulders frequently, they saw no one.

Finally, they rode to the rim of the tabletop that was the edge of Halcyon Valley and over the lip into the slopes of the high desert. Slocum recognized it as Jackrabbit Valley. In the distance he could see the stage road, a faint beige ribbon that cut through cactus, Spanish bayonets, and sagebrush. It was, he thought, one of the most desolate regions he had ever encountered.

Abby picked her way down into a gully thick with

sagebrush and cactus. To Slocum's surprise, there were horses hobbled there, and one end served as a natural corral, with poles to keep the horses from running off. There were watering troughs and hay feeders.

Abby dismounted.

"We'll have to walk back up to the rim," she said. "Another of Wally's precautions."

Slocum swung out of the saddle. They walked to the corral fence. At the other end of the bowl was a natural limestone barrier that blocked off the gully. Some ancient flash flood had hollowed out a portion of the high desert and given shape to the depression. Slocum saw signs of rushing water on either side of the entrance, and a ditch that kept the flooding from entering the gully.

They left their horses saddled and put them inside the makeshift corral.

"You probably won't need your rifle," she said. "Wally gave a great deal of thought to this place and where he found his mine. You'll see."

"I'm already impressed," he said.

The two hiked back up to the rim of the high valley. The ground was rough and rocky, and Abby held Slocum's hand to keep from slipping or falling down when her boots overturned a stone or slid on gravel.

She was breathing hard when they reached the top, and Slocum felt the change in his lungs. The air was thin at that altitude, which he judged to be about seven or eight thousand feet, and the temperature contrast was noticeable. It was slightly warmer in Jackrabbit Valley and cooler now that they were back amid the pines and spruce, the fir and juniper.

"Follow me," she said, and they began a long walk that must have been a mile or more, Slocum figured.

Finally, she stopped between two pine trees. Strung between them was a wire with two empty soup cans hanging close together. She reached up and pulled the wire down. The cans were filled with small pebbles and they rattled.

After that it was quiet for a few minutes as they waited.

Then Slocum saw a man approaching from a thicket of brush and tall trees.

Abby raised a hand and waved.

The man, a Mexican, smiled at her.

"*Hola,* Ruben," she said.

"That's Ruben Vallejo," she said to Slocum, her voice low. "He works for Wally in the mine."

Abby introduced the two men and Ruben shook Slocum's hand.

"Your brother, he is waiting for you, Abby," Ruben said, and walked back in the direction from which he had come. "Watch out for the rattlesnakes," Ruben said as they tramped through thick brush. "I have killed two this morning."

They walked in single file, with Slocum bringing up the rear. Ruben made a lot of noise, shaking the bushes on both sides of him as if to scare away any snakes that might be waiting along the path.

They came into the open and Slocum saw a wide ravine that was deep and long. Pines grew atop the cliffs, and he thought the place would be difficult to find by anyone who did not know where it was.

They entered the ravine and walked some distance to where Wally and another Mexican were standing in front of a pile of debarked logs, leaning against a small ore car on tracks that went into a dark hole at the end of the ravine.

Wally waved. Abby and Slocum waved back.

Slocum noticed that there was a pit filled with shoring some distance away. The superstructure was rigged with ropes and pulleys.

"John," Wally said, a wide grin on his face, "I'm glad you could come. Hi, sis."

The Mexican watched the two men as they embraced in a manly hug.

"John, this is Elisando Gonzalez. You've already met Ruben."

Slocum shook Elisando's hand and the two men smiled at each other.

"As you can see, John, I have two mines here. One going straight into the wall of this ravine, the other straight down into hard rock. That's where I'm seeing the most color."

"This is all a mystery to me, Wally," Slocum said. "I never could understand why men break their backs digging caves and breathing bad air underground."

Wally laughed.

"It's the gold," he said. "When you see it in a pan or in a chunk of ugly rock, it lights up something inside your brain."

"I reckon so," Slocum said.

The two Mexicans walked away. They pushed the ore cart down the tracks and disappeared into the mine adit. Slocum could hear the sound of metal wheels singing along the twin rails.

"It's like a fever, I guess," Wally said. "Maybe like a disease. Once you get gold fever, you lose track of everything else."

"Well, apparently you've stirred up a hornet's nest with your claim, Wally," Slocum said. "Or so Abby tells me."

"It's Cordwainer," Wally said. "He's a madman. He

doesn't have gold fever like the prospectors and miners up here. He just has plain old greed. He'd like to jump my claim, but I've managed to outfox him. So far."

"Wally," Abby said, "I think some of Cordwainer's men murdered Caleb Butterbean last night."

Wally's face fell. His visage turned ashen as if he had been kicked in the stomach.

"Damn," he said. "What happened?"

Abby told him what Sammy had told her.

"And they tried to kill Johnnie last night, too," she said, and told him about the shotgun blasts that tore up his hotel room.

She didn't mention where Slocum had spent the night, but Slocum knew she didn't have to tell him. He knew.

"I've got a line on a couple of the men who came after me," Slocum said. "Same men I saw down on Cactus Flat. You know they murdered Lonnie Taylor. Then burned him after tying him to a juniper tree. I saw them ride off afterwards."

"Lonnie? Oh no, I didn't know," Wally said and he squeezed his eyes shut like tiny fists.

"You know why they killed Lonnie, don't you?" Abby asked her brother.

"I've got a pretty good hunch. Lonnie went crazy over that woman, Ruby Dawson."

"Ruby's a bitch," Abby spat. "She and her bunch of so-called 'golden gals' over at the Jubilee."

"She runs the Jubilee Saloon," Wally explained to Slocum. "Rumor has it that she snares young gals and makes them work for her."

"She makes slaves of them," Abby said.

"Slaves?" Slocum asked.

"Every so often, the stage comes up from Jackrabbit

Valley with a gal or two who answered an ad in some dinky newspaper offering them jobs and maybe marriage. Ruby's one smart woman and I warned Lonnie not to get tangled up with her." Wally kicked a clod of dirt with his work boot, and his eyes closed tight again and squeezed out a tear or two.

"So, Cordwainer's sweet on this Dawson woman," Slocum said.

"I think it's more than that," Wally said. "I think they're in cahoots. And Constable Mayfair is right in there with them. Miners tell me that Ruby and her Golden Gals provide information to Cordwainer about gold strikes and claims. Mayfair will lock some of them up and get more information out of those hapless men. And it all gets back to Cordwainer, who jumps their claims or tortures them to sign over all they have or be hanged on some trumped-up charge Mayfair lays on them."

"It's more than a hornet's nest you've got up here," Slocum said.

"You're damned right it is. That's why I want to run for constable and knock that drunken Mayfair into the middle of next week where he can't do any more harm. Will you help me, John?"

Slocum looked long and hard at his friend. Wally was a lone man in the middle of a snake pit. He was surrounded by greedy and scheming people who had neither morals nor conscience. Halcyon Valley was infected with a disease. It seemed to him that Cordwainer had a strangle hold on the populace of the valley and had managed to ally himself with two dangerous people, Mayfair and Dawson. The constable was probably afraid of Cordwainer, and Ruby Dawson was probably in love with him.

"You know I will, Wally. I don't know how I'm going to do what needs to be done, but it burns me to see a man like Cordwainer wield such power over people. He's like a wormy apple in a barrel full of good ones. He spoils everything he touches."

"You're damned right he does," Wally said. "But, John, I don't want you to risk your life for me. If you think you can run Cordwainer out of the valley without getting yourself killed, it would make this a better place."

"It wouldn't be just for you, Wally, and I don't think Cordwainer is the kind of man who will run from trouble. He seems to have surrounded himself with lawless gunslingers who don't give a damn about human life. I'd stop his clock for you, Abby, Lonnie Foster, Caleb Butterbean, and all the others he's trampled on."

"Whew," Abby exclaimed. "That's the kind of talk I like to hear."

"It's going to be mighty dangerous, John," Wally said. "I couldn't go up against Cordwainer by myself. He'd have his men torture me until I told him where I filed my mining claim or make me sign over all my holdings to him. That's how he operates."

"I'm getting the picture," Slocum said.

He looked at all the pilings, the shoring logs, and a pile of materials covered by a tarp.

"What's under there?" he asked, pointing to the tarp.

"Dynamite, mining tools, caps, fuses. I only blast at night so nobody can see smoke. They might hear the explosions, but they can't tell where I'm blasting."

"So you think these two mines will pay off?" Slocum asked.

"I'm sure of it. Come on, let me show you something."

Abby and Slocum followed Wally as he left the ravine and climbed to the top. He walked to the farthest end and pointed.

"I don't know if you can see it from here," he said, "but if you look close, you can see the big mine over Ettinger Lake."

Slocum could see some of the log superstructure of the Ettinger mine.

"Ettinger is a smart man and he's hired the best mining engineers in California. He thinks he's about to tap into the mother lode and my mines are in a direct line with where he's drilling and blasting."

"I see," said Slocum. The mines were in a direct line with each other. "So Ettinger is coming toward your mine and you're digging toward his."

Wally laughed.

"That's one way of putting it," he said. "When this planet was formed, millions of years ago, there were volcanoes and upheavals. Gold was pure liquid and it flowed like a river down from Alaska, through the Rocky Mountains, and clear to the coast. When the earth cooled, the gold stayed in little pockets, and some of it, the dust, settled in rivers and streams, and we find gold in the tree roots next to a creek and other places. I've found a large vein in the lateral mine and another in the deep rock mine. I believe they're connected, and that the veins go all the way to Ettinger's mine and beyond."

"Could be big, all right," Slocum said.

"Ettinger says that he believes there is a lake of gold right underneath Halcyon Valley," Wally said. "I think he's right."

"But you can't get to it," Slocum said.

"John, you amaze me sometimes. If I had all the

dynamite in the world, I couldn't blast down deep enough to that lake of gold."

"It's that deep, huh?" Slocum said.

"Yes, but the fever keeps me going. Keeps me dreaming. I think there must be some old volcano buried under this mountain and it gushed up the gold I'm finding down there in those two digs."

The three of them walked back down to the ravine. They spoke some more and then Wally said he had to get to work.

"I'll take us back to town," Abby said.

Later, as they were approaching the hotel, Abby said something that stuck in Slocum's mind like a cocklebur under a horse blanket.

"Johnnie," she said, "when you meet Ruby Dawson, and I know you will sooner or later, be careful. She's a witch. And she's very beautiful."

"Beauty is only skin deep," he said.

"I'm serious."

"Except in your case, Abby. Beauty goes all the way through you."

Smiling, she reached over, grabbed his hand, and squeezed it.

They needed no words to express their feelings, but Slocum thought that he was seeing the first wisp of jealousy flashing from Abby's inner fire.

14

The Jubilee Saloon was next door to the Polygon House. It had a gaudy false front with its name emblazoned in gold lettering framed by paintings of two nearly naked voluptuous women whose large eyes seemed to be staring down at passersby on the street.

Below the sign there was this legend: come inside and meet the golden gals!

Slocum noticed that there was a framed walkway leading from the second story to one wing of the hotel.

Very convenient, he thought as he looked up at the two buildings.

There were horses tied to the hitch rail. Slocum had walked there from The Excelsior. Abby had arranged for him to have an inside room to store his possessions and said she would stay at her cabin that night after buying more groceries for her brother. She said she would take these to him the next day and meet him in the afternoon. He was still on the first floor and workmen had repaired his former room, but now he was nearer the lobby and the dining hall and his room had no windows.

Night came quickly in the mountains and it was full dark when Slocum came to the Jubilee. He knew he had to go there and learn all he could, not only about Ruby Dawson, but about the Golden Gals and the patrons, some of whom might be men who worked for Cordwainer.

Two of the horses at the hitch rail interested him. He had seen them before, when the three men on Cactus Flat had ridden off after burning Lonnie Taylor. He looked at the tracks they made as they stood there, hipshot. He struck a match and found clear hoof marks. The two horses were the same ones that had been in the alley when his room had been shotgunned. No mistake about it. He even lifted their hooves to see the distinctive marks they had made in the dirt.

So, he thought, in all likelihood, Hutch and his partner were probably inside the Jubilee. If so, he would have to be very careful and keep them in sight at all times.

There were a dozen horses at the hitch rail. He did not recognize any of the others, but he wasn't checking brands either. The two men who had tried to kill him were there, and that was all he cared about just then.

As he stood outside the saloon, he heard a small band strike up with a lively tune. Music floated out onto the street. Slocum walked toward the batwing doors. Just before he pushed them open, he closed his eyes and took a deep breath.

He pushed both doors aside and strode into the saloon. Men and women were clutching one another and prancing around the dance floor. One or two men at the bar looked his way, then went back to staring at the dancers.

The long bar was on his left and Slocum went to the end of the L where his back would be to the wall. He pulled out a tall stool and sat down. There were two barkeeps on duty. One of them looked over at him and sauntered to his place at the bar.

"Good evenin'," the man said. He wiped a spot on the bar in front of Slocum with a scrap of a towel. "I'm Duke," he said. "What's your pleasure, mister?"

"You have any Kentucky bourbon?" Slocum asked.

"Why, shore. Six bits."

"That's what I'll have then," Slocum said.

"Comin' right up," Duke said and sauntered back down the bar.

Slocum, now that his eyes had adjusted to the dim light inside the saloon, scanned the tables with patrons. He saw women dressed in gold lamé costumes sitting with some of the male customers. One or two were dancing. They wore short skirts, black silk stockings, and tight, low-cut bodices with thin golden stripes from bosom to waist.

Duke brought a bottle of Kentucky's Finest and a shot glass. He poured the glass nearly full and recorked the bottle.

Slocum looked at the label.

"That's a new one on me," he said to the barkeep.

"It's all we have. Don't get much call for bourbon, Kentucky or Tennessee. Mostly whiskey. It's still six bits."

Slocum laid a silver dollar on the bar.

Duke looked at it.

"I'll bring your change," he said.

"Keep it," Slocum said.

"Thanks. Should I leave the bottle?"

"I'll let you know after I have a taste," Slocum said. "Got a glass of water in case I catch fire?"

Duke grinned. "Sure. That'll be two bits extry."

"Like I said, Duke, keep the change after you bring the water."

Duke frowned. He poured water from a pitcher into a tumbler and brought it to Slocum, set it down.

"You just come to town?" Duke asked.

"Yes." Slocum swallowed half of the whiskey and didn't tear up or blink.

"That suit you?"

"It'll do. You can leave the bottle. I might want another."

Duke set the bottle next to the tumbler of water.

"I didn't get your name," the bartender said.

"Didn't give it."

"Is it a secret?"

"The name's Slocum. John Slocum."

"Here on business? Maybe lookin' for gold."

"No. Just moseying around. I came up here for the fresh air."

"Well, we got plenty of that," Duke said. "But if you want more than air, I can have one of the golden gals come over and keep you company."

"That would be fine. Find me the youngest and prettiest, will you, Duke?"

Duke smiled indulgently.

"Sure, that would be Linda Lee. She ain't been here long and she's mighty pretty. Can't be more'n nineteen or twenty."

Slocum downed the rest of his drink and poured another. He set another silver dollar on the bar and watched as Duke beckoned to a girl who was sitting next to the wall as if she were at a town dance and waiting for someone to ask her out onto the floor.

The girl rose up and went to the bar. Duke whispered something to her and pointed to Slocum. She fluffed her blond hair and walked to the end of the bar. Slocum stood up and pulled a stool out for her. He helped her onto it and she smiled at him.

"I'm Linda Lee," she said. "Buy me a drink?"

"I'm John," he said. "What would you like?"

"Duke knows. Just lift a finger and he'll bring it."

Slocum wondered what kind of tea they used for the glitter gals' drinks. Orange Pekoe & Pekoe or some cheap domestic brand.

Duke brought Linda Lee a dark drink with a cherry on a stem dangling down the inside of the glass.

"That'll be two bucks, Mr. Slocum," Duke said, picking up the silver dollar.

Slocum fished out a folded wad of bills, peeled off two ones, and laid them on the bartop.

"I know," Duke said. "Keep the change." There was just the slightest bit of sarcasm to his tone. Slocum poured himself another shot and drank water from his glass.

Linda sipped her drink. It smelled faintly of whiskey, but Slocum knew that it was mostly tea in her glass.

"Where are you from, Linda?" he asked.

"Barstow," she said.

"What brings you to Halcyon Valley?"

"I—uh—I just come up here on the stage. To meet somebody."

"Look," he said, "I'm not the law and I don't work for Cordwainer. I'm just interested in what a nice girl like you is doing in a place like this."

"I get that a lot," she said. "I've only been here a

week, and Miss Ruby, she tells me I got to be nice to the gents who come in here. She pays my room and board and maybe I'll meet a nice feller and go live in Los Angeles one of these days."

"Can you leave anytime you want?"

Linda's face froze as if she had been slapped. "I don't want to talk about it," she said through rigid and tight lips. "Please, mister, I don't want to get in trouble."

"Where do you stay when you're not here?" he asked.

"I have a room at the Polygon," she said.

"What would you charge me if I went to visit you in your room?"

She looked at him, wide-eyed. Her eyes were dark blue, with long groomed lashes. She had an oval face, a pert button nose, and wore a black velvet choker around her neck. She looked very young. And very innocent.

"You have to get your own room at the hotel," she said. "I come to you. It's a sawbuck for an hour, fifty for all night."

"How much of that do you keep, Linda?"

"I give it all to Miss Ruby. She gives me what I need for spending money. She pays for my clothes, manicure, and hairdo. She does that for all the girls."

"Well, do I just tell the desk clerk at the Polygon that I want to see you?"

"Yes. He'll bring me a key to your room. You have to buy whiskey there and pay for one night at least."

Slocum glanced over the room. The small band, which consisted of a fiddler, a guitarist, a drummer, and a bassist, were playing a Viennese waltz, and the song was generating several catcalls from grizzled patrons who wanted them to play something more to their liking.

"Is Ruby Dawson anywhere around?" Slocum asked.

"No. She doesn't usually show up here until after ten or eleven o'clock at night."

"Do you know a man named Hutch?" he asked.

Again, that frozen look on Linda's face.

"I don't know him," she said, her voice pitched low, "but I know who he is."

"Is he here?" Slocum asked. "You don't have to point, just tell me where he might be sitting."

"He's here," she whispered. She looked down the bar to see if anyone was close enough to hear her. "He come in with a man named Joe Creek. If you look in the far corner, over to the right, you might see them. They're drinking beer and smoking cigarettes. I think they're waiting for somebody."

"What makes you think that?"

"They asked Duke if somebody named Cory had come in yet. Duke told them no and they walked back to that table and ordered beers. They ain't been here long."

"Do you know this Cory they asked about?"

"Just that he works for Mr. Jess Cordwainer. His name's Cory Windom, I think. He don't come in here much."

"Did you know Lonnie Taylor?" Slocum asked.

Linda's body jerked as if she had been electrocuted. She reared back on her stool and blinked her eyes several times.

"Mr. Slocum, you ask too many questions. Are you sure you ain't the law?"

"I'm not the law," he said. "I just wondered if you had met or knew Lonnie Taylor."

"I—I can't talk about that."

"He's dead, you know," Slocum said.

Linda became very nervous. Her hand shook when she lifted her glass. She looked as if she wanted to run and never stop running.

She lowered her head and then looked up at Slocum.

"You kin to Lonnie?" she asked.

"No. I didn't know him. But I saw him burn up like a human torch down on Cactus Flat. Three men rode away from there. One of them was Hutch. He's the man I want to see."

"He—He'll kill you," she whispered, so low he could barely hear her.

"Why do you say that?"

"Because of what the other women here have said about him. They knew that something was going to happen to Lonnie. He kept coming here and sparking Miss Ruby. That's all I know. Somebody told him to stay away from Miss Ruby, but he didn't listen."

Just then, Slocum saw one of the men sitting at that back corner table get up and start walking toward him. From his gait, from the way he carried himself, Slocum knew who it was.

"Linda, you'd better find another place to sit and finish your drink," he said.

"Why, don't you favor me no more?"

"I think I'm going to be busy in a few minutes."

She followed his gaze and a hand flew to her mouth.

"Oh dear," she said. "That's Hutch."

She scooted off the stool and carried her drink to the row of chairs next to the wall where she had been sitting.

Hutch didn't seem to have noticed Slocum. He was angling toward the doorway at the far end of the bar. He was probably going to relieve himself, Slocum thought.

He sipped from his glass and watched as Hutch walked past several tables.

Then Hutch stopped suddenly and looked straight at Slocum.

Slocum returned the stare and smiled. Then he touched two fingers to the brim of his hat in a brief, somewhat mocking salute.

Hutch's face twisted into a scowl as Slocum kept smiling at him.

But his eyes had narrowed to slits and his jawline had turned as hard as chiseled stone.

15

The waltz ended and the band struck up the first strains of "Camptown Races." Laughter filled the room and cheers rose up from the bearded prospectors and hard-rock miners at the tables.

Hutch changed directions and walked slowly toward Slocum.

Slocum swung the top of the stool around so that he was facing the gunman. His right hand was free and his own pistol hung at his side, within easy reach.

Hutch continued to walk toward Slocum, that same scowl plastered to his face like a dark scab.

"You're Slocum, ain't ye?" Hutch said as he halted about ten feet away.

"That's right, Hutch."

Hutch flinched slightly at the mention of his name.

"You got no business here in Halcyon Valley, Slocum. And from what I hear, you're wanted for murder back in Georgia."

"Rumors are everywhere these days," Slocum said.

"I think you ought to clear out before something bad happens to you," Hutch said.

Slocum slid off the stool and stood with his legs apart a foot or two.

"I saw something this afternoon that makes me want to stay," Slocum said.

"Yeah? What's that?" Hutch appeared belligerent. He was no longer scowling, but he held his right hand a few inches above the pistol on his belt.

"I saw a dead mule, Hutch."

"A dead mule?" Hutch's face went blank.

"That's right. I was riding out to see a pard of mine and there were buzzards circling in the sky and I rode up on a bunch of them tearing into a dead mule."

"That's just too damned bad, Slocum. Dead mules don't mean nothin'."

"Oh, this one means a lot. I looked at him real close and he was full of buckshot."

"Mules die. People die. 'Specially if they don't have no sense."

"On the road, I saw a bunch of boot tracks. I looked at those, too."

"Folks walk. They wear boots. They leave tracks. What are you drivin' at?"

"I saw those same tracks outside the window of my hotel room and in the alley. Same horse tracks, too. And outside here, those same two horses that left tracks where the mule was shot and in the alley behind the hotel. Makes me think you might be a bushwhacker, Hutch."

Hutch stiffened. His hand dropped another inch or two toward the butt of his pistol. His eyes narrowed to slits and his lips clamped together over a jutting chin.

"You accusin' me of somethin', Slocum?"

"No. I'm just here to remind you of the bill you owe."

"I don't owe no bill. Leastwise, not to you."

"No, you don't owe me anything, Hutch," Slocum said, the shadow of a smile flickering on his face. "But you owe the Piper."

"The Piper?"

"Yes." Slocum's right hand did not move, but it was waist high, in a direct line with his own holstered .45. It hovered there like a hawk in a painting, motionless, but open and ready to dive and pull his pistol.

"I don't know what in hell you're talkin' about," Hutch spat, more annoyed than angry.

"Well, you know the Piper has to be paid."

"Huh?" There was that blank look of puzzlement on Hutch's face again.

"The Piper has to be paid. You killed Lonnie Taylor, Caleb Butterbean. You tried to kill me. And you killed his mule, Josie."

"You're full of bull crap, Slocum."

"I'm here to collect for the Piper, Hutch. Make your move or I'll drop you where you stand."

"Why, you dumb sonofabitch," Hutch said and his hand dropped to the butt of his pistol. His hand closed around the wooden grip.

Slocum's hand dove toward his own pistol. His movement was so fast, his hand was just a blur. Before Hutch had cleared his pistol from its holster, Slocum's Colt was level at his hip and aimed straight at Hutch.

Hutch heard the click as Slocum thumbed the hammer back all in one smooth motion.

The band stopped playing.

The card games stopped.

Dancers froze on the dance floor.

Every head was turned toward the two men facing each other.

The click of the hammer engaging the trigger mechanism was like a thunderclap in the silence of the saloon.

Duke froze, a glass and towel in his hand.

The other bartender, whose name was Russ Cooley, never set the glass of beer in his hand down on the bar and swallowed silently as his body turned as rigid as a statue.

Joe Creek stood up in the back of the room and tried to see what was happening.

All he saw was Hutch's back and that he was facing a man in the shadows at the end of the bar.

Slocum held his breath and squeezed the trigger.

His Colt bucked against the palm of his right hand. Sparking powder, bright orange streaks, spurted from the barrel of his six-gun, followed by a cloud of white smoke. His thumb hammered back before the bullet struck Hutch in the center of his chest.

The barrel of Hutch's gun was still inside the top of the holster when the lead ball struck his breastbone, shattering it like a brittle piece of crockery. A black hole appeared next to a button on his shirt, and blood, lung blood, spurted through that hole and drenched his striped shirt. His knees collapsed and he sank to the floor, his mouth opened to scream as blood gushed up his throat and spewed through his teeth in a thick red spray. His eyes glazed over as he appeared to be staring at Slocum in surprise. He tumbled forward onto his face and twitched a couple of times and then lay still, not breathing, dead as a stone.

Slocum eased the hammer of his pistol down to half-cock but did not holster it.

He looked, instead, at the crowd and beyond to the far right corner of the saloon.

Joe Creek felt all alone and exposed.

Slocum stepped forward and stood under one of the candlelit chandeliers, where he knew his face could be seen by all who were there.

He raised his left hand and beckoned to Joe Creek.

"Creek," Slocum said in a loud deep voice that carried clear across the room, "I opened the ball. You want to dance?"

Creek's face blanched. He went to the window and pulled it open. As everyone watched, he climbed through the opening and vanished into the night.

Slocum ran to the door, sprang through the batwings. He knew where Creek's horse was tied.

But Creek was not there.

Instead, Slocum saw him running down the street, a shadow in the darkness.

He called after him.

"You can run, Creek," Slocum shouted, "but I'll track you straight to your grave."

The shadow disappeared into heavier shadows and Slocum holstered his pistol.

He walked over to the two horses owned by Creek and Hutch. He slid a sawed-off shotgun from the scabbard of one horse, then removed the one from the other horse.

Then he walked over to the circle of stones around the arrastre and bashed first one barrel and then the other on the rocks until the barrels were bent and crushed. He threw them into the center of the arrastre, where there was a large hole filled with crushed rocks.

Then he walked next door to the Polygon and entered it as if he had not a care in the world.

The desk clerk looked up at him.

"I heard shots from the saloon next door," the clerk said. "What's goin' on over there?"

"Somebody just paid the Piper," Slocum said.

The clerk, a man in his forties who looked as if he had missed more than one meal at the chuck wagon, stood there, his sallow face twisted in puzzlement.

Slocum pulled out a fifty-dollar bill and laid it on the counter.

"I want a room and I want Linda Lee," he said. "Pronto. And I'm not signing your register and you don't know who I am or what room I'm in. You got that?"

"Yes, sir. It's highly irregular, but there's some who can't sign their names and—"

"If anybody but Linda Lee opens my door, you're going to hear more gunshots."

"Yes, that will be ten dollars. I'll get your change."

"And you'd better give me a bottle of whiskey to take up with me."

"Yes, sir. Twenty dollars. A double sawbuck."

"Take it out of the fifty and give me the change."

The clerk bent down and opened a cabinet. He took out a bottle of whiskey. It was not Kentucky bourbon, but Slocum didn't care. He wasn't going to drink any of it.

"I don't want to be disturbed by anybody but Linda Lee," he told the clerk. "Or you'll pay the Piper yourself." He really had no intention of harming the quivering man, but he had made his point.

The clerk, one Jasper Naylor, gulped and set a key on the counter with the rest of the unspent bills.

Slocum took his change and a key to one of the upstairs rooms, number 45. The clerk told him which wing it was in and Slocum ascended the stairs.

He heard the band strike up again as he walked to

his room. Somehow, the music did not seem as lively or joyous, and instead of a guitar, he heard the plink of a banjo.

Life goes on, he thought as he unlocked the door to his room and went inside. For some of us anyway.

He lit the lamp that was on the center table. There was another next to the bed, but he left it unlit.

He locked the door and waited. The music, lackluster and dreary, drifted up to his room through the window.

He wondered if Linda Lee would show up after what had happened.

If not, so be it.

He set the whiskey bottle on the dresser and stretched out on the bed.

When he heard the key turn in the lock, he sat up.

The door opened.

Very slowly.

A woman stepped inside.

The woman was not Linda Lee.

She was someone Slocum had never seen before.

But she was so beautiful, he was sure his heart had stopped beating.

"Hello, John Slocum," the woman said. "I'm Ruby Dawson. I hope you don't mind that Linda Lee couldn't come. She's indisposed."

With that, Ruby turned and locked the door.

She dropped the key on the table and strode toward Slocum.

"No charge for my visit," she said, her voice low and husky. "In fact, from what I see of you, I may pay you."

Slocum was sure his heart had stopped as she approached him. She was all black lace and red trim with a gold beret in her sleek black hair. She had an hourglass figure and her long dress was slit on both sides so that her legs flashed, legs encased in silk mesh stockings that gleamed like satin in the lamplight.

The music from the saloon faded and Slocum's scalp prickled as he caught the scent of Ruby's heady perfume and the faint musk of her as she stopped in front of him and put slender hands on his cheeks, then bent down and kissed him before he could brace himself.

She made a low moan in her throat and Slocum felt the rush of blood to his loins.

Then she grasped the swelling lump of his manhood and kneaded it between her fingers until it grew and hardened into a thick torpedo that stretched his crotch to the breaking point.

16

Ruby Dawson patted the bulge in Slocum's trousers and took a small step backward.

Her dark brown eyes glittered as she looked directly into Slocum's. His green eyes took on a glazed cast as he stared at Ruby's unblemished face, her elegant patrician nose, firm pointed chin, and ample bosom. She was tall, with radiant black hair, slender arms and legs. She wore little makeup, just a touch of vermilion rouge on her cheeks, a light red hue on her lips, and a dusting of mascara on her long eyelashes.

"Your little man is easily aroused," she said, staring down at Slocum's crotch. "I think he wants to get out."

"I think he wants to get out and then get into something," Slocum husked.

"Let's free him together," she said, and dropped to her knees. She knelt in front of Slocum and inched to a place between his legs. Her long delicate fingers began to unbutton his fly, expertly working the buttons through the slits. She reached in and drew his cock out of his undershorts. It sprang to attention like the stalk of some exotic plant that grew out of a matted jungle.

"My, my," she cooed, "he's a dandy."

She stroked the crown of his cock, the velvet head that appeared when she stripped back the foreskin.

She stroked his organ up and down, then bent over and lightly kissed the smooth warhead. Slocum felt a streak of electricity shoot through his loins, and it took every bit of mental effort to keep from shooting his seed right then and there.

"Oh, I almost got you to spurt, John. We wouldn't want to waste it now, would we?"

"The little guy has a mind of his own," Slocum said. "He's hard to manage sometimes."

"Well, I've toyed with him long enough. I must have him for my treasure chest. Is that all right with you, Mr. Slocum?"

"He goes where he's needed," Slocum said.

"I like that," Ruby said. "Is he always on call then?"

"He stands ready to obey your bidding, pretty lady."

"Call me Ruby," she said. "The name matches my lips, don't you think?"

"Which ones?" Slocum asked, flashing her a wry smile.

"Oh, you. You have a sense of humor, I see."

Slocum said nothing as she stepped back from the bed and started slipping out of her dress. He began to unbutton his shirt. He bared his chest and pulled off his black shirt while she worked her panties down her long legs. She stepped out of her shoes, but did not take off her silk mesh stockings, which were attached to a black lace garter belt. Slocum took off his gun belt, but did not wrap the cartridges around his holster. He lifted a pillow and placed his rig underneath it. He unbuttoned the top button of his trousers as he worked his stovepipe boots off. They hit the floor with a couple of dull thumps and he pulled his pants down and left them in a puddle atop his boots.

Ruby stood before him, fully naked except for her black stockings and garter belt. She stepped up to him and pulled off his undershorts. He stiffened his legs and she tossed the garment atop his pants.

"Must you have your pistol in the same bed with us?" she asked as Slocum scooted to the other side to make room for her.

"You never know who might come through that door next," he said. "I was expecting Linda Lee and you showed up. Could be there's still another key down at the desk."

"Well, we won't worry about that now, will we?"

Ruby slid into bed next to Slocum and enveloped him with her arms. He clasped her in a strong embrace and the two kissed. It was a long and lingering kiss and he felt her tongue exploring the inside of his mouth. He inched his own tongue into her mouth and the two engaged in loving oral combat, their tongues probing and lashing at one another's as if they were blind fencers.

He rolled over on top of her and they broke the kiss as she spread her legs. Her hand reached down and grasped his rock-hard stalk and guided it to her labia. She guided him through the portal and he slid inside her, laved with the hot juices of her cunt.

Ruby sighed and dug fingernails into his back as he penetrated deeper. He moved in and out of her with slow, smooth stroking. The warmth inside increased and the juices flowed. She pushed upward with her hips as he lowered his own. They smacked together like a pair of flounders on the beach and the bedsprings rang with the intensity of their bodies' thrashings.

"It's good, John," she moaned. "So very, very good. You could hire out as a stud."

"In your stable?" he said.

Ruby laughed. It was a mirthful laugh husky with lust. He pushed in hard, and her body bucked with a shuddering orgasm. She opened her mouth and let out a soft scream as her fingernails dug into his back with the intensity of her climax.

"What makes you think I have a stable?"

"All the Golden Girls. Don't they work for you?"

"No, they don't work for me, John. I'm like a house mother to them."

"You're too young to be a house mother."

Ruby laughed and bucked beneath him.

"They're mostly ignorant waifs who have lost their way," Ruby said. "I see to it that they bathe and dress properly, are fed and made to look nice."

"And you give them jobs as glitter gals," he said.

"You've got it all wrong," she said. "The Jubilee Saloon hires them until they get on their feet and perhaps find husbands."

He stroked her slow and deep and Ruby responded with matching undulations. It felt good to be inside her, to see her eyes shine and her body respond to his plunging cock.

"And who owns the Jubilee?" he asked.

"Why, Jess Cordwainer owns the saloon and this hotel, why?"

"So, Cordwainer is your boss?"

"Yes. He takes care of me," she said.

"Are you in love with him?" Slocum asked bluntly.

Ruby stiffened for a split second. Then she ground her hips in a circular motion.

"He thinks I am," she moaned.

"But you're not."

"My, you ask the most delicate questions, John. Delicate and personal. I work for Jess. He doesn't own me. He hasn't put a ring on my finger."

No, Slocum thought, but he's put a ring through your nose and leads you around like a trained monkey. He was forming a picture of Ruby in his mind. She seemed to be an ambitious woman who was drawn to powerful men like Cordwainer. She feathered her own nest and, like Cordwainer, seemed not to have any empathy for other people. As long as they were making money and there was a chance to make more from innocent people, they were happy. And they would thrive. Ruby was no better than Cordwainer or the men he hired. She was a hired gun herself, only she preyed on young women, teaching them things they should have learned from decent men, not in a saloon or whorehouse.

Suddenly, he began to lose all desire for Ruby's body. She hadn't come to his room out of passion or personal interest in him, but to seduce him for her own, and Cordwainer's, gain.

He stopped pumping in and out of Ruby's sheath. He started to pull out when she grabbed his hips and pulled him hard against her.

"What's wrong?" she asked. "You're not finished yet."

"Yes I am, Ruby."

"But I want your seed. I want you to shoot your jism inside me. I want you to feel what I feel."

"It's useless," he said. "I've lost all feeling for you."

Her face contorted in anger.

"Why, you bastard," she said. "How dare you stop right in the middle of something good."

"It's not good anymore, Ruby."

He pushed her arms down and withdrew. That was when Ruby turned into a fighting tigress. She flailed both arms, striking his shoulders with her hands. He backed off her and slid from the bed. His penis lost its rigidity and she looked at him with contempt and fury.

Then she turned over and her hands slid under his pillow. She dragged his holster and gun belt out and started to draw his .45.

Slocum stepped over to her and jerked the rig from her hands. She kicked him in the crotch and he doubled over in pain.

"You bastard," she hissed, seething with fury.

"Lady, you've worn out your welcome. Now get dressed and walk out of here or I'll kick you out buck naked."

"You lousy sonofabitch," Ruby spat. "I gave you my body and this is the thanks I get."

"Your body's not worth much," he said. "It's been around the horn too many times."

He stepped away, picked up her clothes, and threw them on the bed. She kicked and thrashed, her face livid with anger.

Slocum reached down and picked up his shorts and pulled them on while Ruby glared at him.

"No man has ever done this to me, Slocum," she said as she began to dress while still lying down.

"Then, it's about time," he said. He finished dressing and strapped on his gun belt. Then he filched a cheroot from his pocket, stuck it in his mouth, and lit it as he sat down at the table to watch Ruby finish dressing.

"You'll pay for killing Al Hutchins," she warned as

she stalked over to him. "You shot him down in cold blood."

"He was drawing his own pistol when I shot him," Slocum corrected her.

"Constable Mayfair will have you locked up before you can say 'Jack Robinson,'" she sneered.

"You know where the door is, Ruby. Get your ass out of here before I throw you out."

She snorted and walked to the door.

He watched as she turned the key. She went out and he heard her heavy footsteps as she stomped down the hall.

Slocum waited several minutes. He smoked his cheroot down to the halfway mark, then got up and left the room.

He had found out what he needed to know without Linda Lee providing him with her services.

The more he thought about the Jubilee and the Polygon House and the stranglehold that Cordwainer had on the town, the more determined Slocum was to go after him and his men. He would either drive them out of Halcyon Valley or kill them.

First on his list was Joe Creek. Slocum knew what he looked like and he knew which horse he rode.

He shouldn't be hard to find.

Slocum didn't see anyone at the desk when he walked down to the lobby. He tossed his key on the counter and went out the back door.

It was a good thing that he did, for waiting just outside the hotel, in the shadows, were two men, their pistols drawn and cocked.

They were both looking through the front windows of the hotel.

"Who was that?" Cory Windom asked when they

saw a man throw a key on the counter then walk away down the hall to the back door. "Was that Slocum?"'

Joe Creek nodded and let out a breath.

"It sure looked like the bastard," he said. "Black hat, black shirt, black pants."

"Damn. He outsmarted us, Joe."

"I reckon he ain't goin' to be easy to kill, Cory."

"Well, we can't go chasin' him down the alley this time of night. It's pitch dark and he might just be waitin' for us."

"We'll get him some other time," Creek said.

"You should have braced him when he was in the Jubilee."

Creek shook his head.

"You didn't see what I saw, Cory. When he killed Hutch, he was just as cool and smooth as a coiled snake."

"Well, if he's a snake, we got to take a hoe to that bastard and cut off his head."

"Ruby wants his balls cut off," Creek said.

"Fuck Ruby," Windom scoffed.

"I think Slocum already did," Creek remarked.

Windom laughed and holstered his pistol.

Music from the Jubilee poured into the street. The band was playing "Polly Wolly Doodle."

The street was empty.

Halcyon Valley was full of ghosts and a man dressed all in black.

17

The Jubilee Saloon was closed at that hour of the morning. The sun was shining on the snow-capped peaks of the mountains, but the little village of Halcyon Valley was still filled with shadows, and the air still bore the night chill. The arrastre was silent and deserted while the rest of the town seemed abandoned of all life, except for the Valley General Store, where Mexicans were unloading groceries hauled up from Grizzly Lake during the night.

Inside the Jubilee, Cordwainer sat at one of the tables, his cold eyes glaring at the two men who sat opposite him. All had cups of steaming coffee in front of them. Nearby, at another table, sat Ruby Dawson, dipping a teaspoonful of sugar into her cup. A cigarette was burning in the tin ashtray next to her cup, and her eyes were as cold as Cordwainer's.

Lou Jessup toyed with a .45-caliber bullet, while Pat

Morris blew steam from the rim of his coffee cup before taking his first sip.

"We've got a wolf in our sheep camp," Cordwainer said. He bit off the end of a fat cigar and stuck the other end in his mouth. He picked up a match, struck it on the sandpaper strip glued to the side of the matchbox. He lit his cigar and drew on it. A wreath of blue smoke encircled his hatless head. "Slocum has made fools of us, and he's only been here a couple of days."

"Well, Joe should have stood up to him," Jessup said. "He's a damned coward."

"And what about Windom? He stood outside the hotel with Joe last night and let Slocum walk right out of the hotel," Morris said.

"Mistakes were made," Cordwainer said. "No doubt about it. I thought Hutch would have more sense, but he let himself get shot dead in front of everybody who was here last night."

Then he turned to Ruby, who was sipping her coffee.

"And you," he said, "you should have taken that little .38 up to Slocum's room and put his lamp out. Instead, you let the bastard—"

"Jess," she said, setting her cup down on the table, "I didn't know anything about John Slocum when I went up there. Only that he had shot Hutch and I wanted to find out what made his clock tick."

"And did you?" Cordwainer snarled. His eyes bulged out and the veins in his neck strained against his skin like purple worms burrowing through sand.

"He's a dangerous man, I grant you, Jess. I'd hate to go up against him."

"But you did go up against him, Ruby, like the slut you are."

She jerked her head back as if she had been slapped.

There were dark circles under her eyes and they all could tell she had been crying.

"I made a mistake. Like you said. I thought I could charm him, make him tell me what he was doing up here in the valley."

"You know what I think?" Cordwainer said.

Ruby, Lou, and Pat all looked at him with blank faces.

Finally, Lou said, "What's that, boss?"

"I think Slocum came up here because he was invited. Someone, some bastard, sent for him, and I think I know who it was."

"Who?" Ruby asked, her voice scratching from taking a drag on her cigarette.

"Wally Newman. Nobody's seen hide nor hair of him in weeks. His sister, Abigail, knows where he is and I think, no, I know damned well she's carryin' food and such out to wherever he's holed up."

"We follered that gal all over," Pat said, "and she always gives us the slip."

"Well, you're going to follow her again, Pat, and you, Lou, and find out where Newman is hiding. And maybe you'll find his claim while you're at it."

"So when do we do that?" Lou asked. "Hell, she was gone the other day and we couldn't even track her."

"Mayfair just left here ten minutes before you came. He camped out at her cabin last night and then followed her to Canby's General Store. She's riding that dun. Herb's back at the store now, waiting for Arnie Canby to open up. He's sure she's going to buy food and pack it out to her brother's digs."

"Herb's going to follow her?" Pat asked.

"No, you goose. You and Lou are. But you've got to be real careful this time. Split up, and if she sees one of you, the other'n will take up her trail. I want you both to find Wally Newman and bring him back here."

"And if we don't?" Lou asked.

"You get that woman. Tie her up and bring her to me at my cabin. Either she'll tell me where her brother is holed up, or he'll come looking for her."

"You want us to maybe kidnap that Abigail woman?" Pat said.

There was a silence as Cordwainer glared at the two men.

"If you don't bring either Wally or Abigail back today, then don't come back here yourselves. If you do, and you're empty-handed, I'll shoot you myself, or tell Windom to put lead in your damned bellies."

"Jesus, boss, that's pretty harsh," Pat said.

"Slocum is a thorn in my side. Windom and Creek are lookin' for him up here, but in case they don't find him and kill him, next best thing is to haul Wally and his sister back up here. Slocum will have hell to pay getting to me at my cabin. He'll run into a storm of bullets if he even comes near all them rocks on Union Flat."

Cordwainer drained his coffee cup and slammed the cup down on the table. The sound of the tin striking wood made the others jump in their chairs.

He blew smoke at Lou and Pat, and another stream in Ruby's direction.

He balled up his fists.

"Do I make myself clear?" Cordwainer said.

"Yeah, you do," Pat said.

"Real perfect-like," Lou said.

"Now, get on your horses and down to Canby's. You stay out of sight and track that gal to Wally's digs. If you find his claim, I'll pay you a bonus of one hundred dollars apiece."

"What about if we bring him and his sis back?" Lou asked. "Do we get a bonus?"

"Yeah," Cordwainer grumbled, "half that. Fifty bucks apiece."

"Well, shit fire," Pat said, "let's get to it, Lou."

Both men got up and left the saloon. They took long strides to go out the back door, where their saddled horses were hitched to a post.

Ruby picked up her cup and moved over to the table vacated by the two men.

"You think they'll find Newman?" she asked.

"I don't know. He's pretty cagey. But if not, they'd better bring that girl back here. She's the bait."

"The bait?"

"Yeah, like honey to a bear, Ruby. If I've got her, either Newman or Slocum will come after her. It don't matter which."

"You know, Jess," she said. "You're a pretty smart man. Maybe the smartest I've ever known."

"And you, Ruby," he said, "you're the prettiest whore I ever saw."

"Don't call me that," she snapped at him. "Don't you ever call me a whore."

"I'll call you whatever I want, Ruby, and you know it," he said.

She dipped her head and struggled to hold back the tears as she squeezed both eyes shut.

Cordwainer shot her a scornful look and pushed away from the table.

"But I like you, Ruby," he said before he walked away. "I like you a lot."

He left her there and walked out through the back door.

"You bastard," Ruby muttered. "You dirty rotten bastard."

Then crumpling, she laid her head on the table and began to cry.

Sunlight streamed through the windows, and dust motes danced like fireflies in the beams. The sound of her sobbing was the only sign of life in the empty saloon.

18

Canby finished totaling up the figures for Abby while she stuffed canned goods, fresh celery, onions, beans, and tobacco into her oversized saddlebags on the counter.

"Not so much this time," he said. He was a blubbery little fat man with at least three chins and a bloated tire around his belly. He was balding and wore small rimless eyeglasses that rested on his mushroom nose. His wife helped him in the store since he couldn't afford to hire outside help on his meager business earnings. They had come out from Iowa and found too much competition both in San Bernardino and Grizzly Lake, so they had taken over a failed business in a log building in Halcyon Valley. His wholesaler down in San Bernardino shipped his orders up by wagon every two weeks.

Abby opened her purse and drew out several bills. She peeled off a twenty and handed it to Canby.

"I'll get your change," he said.

He walked to the cash register, pressed some buttons

that showed the amount in a small glass window. He put the bill in the drawer and took out two one-dollar bills, a quarter, a dime, and two pennies.

"There you are, Miss Abby," he said.

"Thanks, Mr. Canby."

"You in some kind of trouble?" Canby asked.

"Not that I know of. Why?"

"I saw you through the shutters when you rode up on that dun horse of yours. I started to go to the back and supervise the unloading of the supply wagon, but something caught my eye."

"Oh?" Abby's eyebrows arched as she stuffed the change back in her purse.

"I saw Constable Mayfair on his horse. He looked like he was following you. I thought he might ride up to the hitch rail, but he stopped down the street for a minute, then rode off toward the north end of town, where the Polygon and Jubilee are."

"I didn't see him. Are you sure he was following me?"

"You and he were the only ones I saw. And a little later, I saw him again. He rode up between two buildings across the street. Like he was hiding or something."

"Hmm. Sounds very mysterious."

"Miss Abby, when I looked again, he was standin' just inside the shadows twixt them two buildings, just a-watchin' the front of my store and your horse out there."

"Are you sure, Mr. Canby?"

"Sure. So before you go, I think I'll take another look if you don't mind. You stay right where you are."

She turned toward the door and the front window. Canby walked to the shutters and opened them slightly.

He looked both ways up the street, then closed the shutters and walked back to where Abby waited.

"He seems to be gone, Miss Abby."

"Good," she said. "I hope the constable found what he was looking for."

"Did you hear the news?" he asked. "What happened last night up at the Jubilee?"

"Why no, Mr. Canby. What happened?"

"There was a shooting. A man was killed."

"Oh? Who? Do you know?"

"They said it was a man who worked for Mr. Cordwainer. I think his name was Hutchins. They're buryin' him and poor Caleb Butterbean out to the cemetery today."

"That's interesting," she said as she hefted the saddlebags off the counter. "Who shot Hutch?"

"I dunno. Some stranger. He was all dressed in black. Soon as Hutchins was dead, he lit a shuck."

"Thank you, Mr. Canby. That was no great loss."

"No'm, it wasn't, I reckon."

She walked outside and looked around before loading her saddlebags in back of her saddle. She saw no one. She unwrapped her reins and stepped into her saddle. She looked up and down the street, but saw no other person at that hour. The sun had cleared the high peaks and was scraping away the puddles of shadows from the foundations of some of the buildings. She raised the collar of her jacket to block the breeze from blowing on her neck.

She turned the dun away from the hitch rail and rode up the street so that she would pass the constable's small office. She felt satisfied when she saw Mayfair's horse at the hitch rail out front. Nothing to worry about, she thought. She guided her horse past the arrastre, into the open. She looked back when she reached a fringe of timber. The town gleamed brown and gray in the rising sun and seemed deserted.

"Nothing to worry about," she said to herself as she waited in the timber and looked back toward town.

But she had an uneasy feeling as she set out on her long circuitous route to her brother's cabin.

Something was wrong, but she couldn't put her finger on it.

And who was the man who'd shot and killed Hutch?

A man in black.

It could be no other than Johnnie Slocum.

She hoped it was her Johnnie who had killed Hutch.

But where was he?

She missed him.

And maybe, she thought, she was falling in love with him. She had loved him before, but as a little girl. Now that she was a woman, it was different.

The longing she felt was deeper now and layered with feelings she didn't fully understand.

As she rode deeper into the timber, she thought of him and wished he were with her now.

She almost turned back, but did not.

It would turn out to be a big mistake.

19

At first, Slocum thought the faint taps and the scratching existed only in his dream. He heard them while he slept, but the sounds fit perfectly into his dreamscape.

In the dream, Slocum was deep in a cave. He heard rats scurrying about as he attempted to climb out of the shaft. There was a heavy iron door at the top of the tunnel. On the other side, he could see wolves clawing to get in. He saw them through cracks in the door.

The wolves had large teeth and their jaws dripped saliva and blood. He saw the long claws on their paws as they stood on their hind legs and savagely scraped at the door.

The door burst open and a pack of wolves flew at him.

Slocum opened his eyes, jarred out of sleep by the vividness of the dream.

At first he did not know where he was. The sun was up, its light shimmering beneath the door.

He realized that he was in The Excelsior Hotel, and that there was something scratching and tapping on his door.

He grabbed the butt of his pistol from beneath his pillow and swung off the bed.

He hammered back and approached the door at an angle so that if anyone fired through the door he would not be struck by the bullets.

"Who's there?" he called.

He heard a croak that he could not distinguish as a word.

"Who?" he asked again.

"S-Sammy," the voice croaked.

"Sammy?"

"Please. Let me in."

Slocum stood at the side of the door and lifted the latch. The door opened inward and he saw Sammy slumped down on the sunlit carpet, his face bruised, his nose dripping blood.

"Mr. Slocum, I didn't tell them," Sammy groaned. It was obvious that the hotel clerk was in pain.

Slocum set his pistol down and lifted Sammy into the room. He carried him to the bed and laid him out atop the cover. He went back to the door, locked it, and picked up his cocked .45.

He holstered his pistol as Sammy moaned in pain.

"Don't try to talk, Sammy," Slocum said. "I'm going to clean you up and see how bad you're hurt."

Slocum quickly tugged on his trousers and slipped into his shirt. He pulled on his boots and walked to the bureau. He found small towels in a drawer, and he took one of these, set it in the porcelain bowl, and poured water on it. He wrung it out and carried it to the bed.

He swabbed the blood off Sammy's face and from

under his nose. He saw small gouges in his scalp. They looked like wounds a man would get from a pistol whipping. He opened Sammy's shirt and saw dark bluish-purple bruises on both sides of his chest.

"What happened to you, Sammy?" he asked. "Who did this to you?"

"I didn't tell 'em, Mr. Slocum," Sammy said. His voice was weak and full of gravel as if someone had punched him in the Adam's apple.

"What didn't you tell them, Sammy?"

"I—I didn't tell 'em where you was. They—they beat me, but I told them you weren't here."

"Who? Who beat you, Sammy?"

Sammy struggled to sit up, but Slocum pushed him back down. He laid the wet cloth across his forehead and felt his cheeks to see if he was running a fever.

"They beat you pretty bad, Sammy. Want me to see if I can get you a doc? Is there even one up here in the valley?"

"No—no, I—I'll be all right. I hurt all over, but I didn't tell them nothin', Mr. Slocum. I think they meant to kill you."

"Do you know who they were? Their names?"

"I know their names. I know who they work for. They're mean men, Mr. Slocum. Some say they kill just for the fun of it."

"Names, Sammy. I need their names."

"One of 'em is Joe Creek. The other'n is Cory Windom. Bad men."

"Don't you worry about them, Sammy. Can you get someone to take your place at the desk?"

"No. Ain't many can do what I do. But I'm going to pack a pistol from now on. I have one at home."

"Want to borrow my sawed-off?"

Sammy shook his head.

"No, sir. I'm feelin' a tad better after talkin' to you. I didn't tell them nothin'."

Slocum took the towel from the boy's forehead and felt his cheeks again.

"You're going to have a headache for a day or two, Sammy. You need to put some iodine on those cuts on your head."

"I got an aid kit in the hotel office."

"I'm going after those men, Sammy. I don't like what they did to you, and you're dead right. They are out to kill me."

"You better be real careful, Mr. Slocum. They don't play fair. They get the chance, they'll shoot you in the back."

"I know what kind of men they are, Sammy. Don't you worry about me."

Slocum helped Sammy to the front desk. Then he got his bedroll, saddlebags, and rifle from his room, locked it, and left the key at the desk.

"If I'm not back for a day or two," he told Sammy, "don't worry. I'll be tracking those men who beat you up."

"I wish Miss Abby was here," he said.

"She'll be back this afternoon or tomorrow, I reckon."

"I don't know," Sammy said. "When I come to work this mornin', I saw her ride past the constable's office, then out of town. Her saddlebags was bulgin', so I figure she was goin' to see her brother. Wherever he is."

"Yes, she was," Slocum said.

"Right after she rode off, I saw two more of Cordwainer's men ride off after her. I didn't think much of it at the time, but after what happened to me, I ain't so sure."

"What do you mean?"

"I know Cordwainer wants to jump Wally's claim and she says his men try to foller her whenever she takes groceries to Wally. But I never saw anyone go after her here in town before."

Slocum drew in a deep breath.

Now that he was in town, Cordwainer was upping the ante. He wanted that mining claim of Wally's and he was ruthless enough to go after Abby, perhaps torture her to reveal where Wally's mine was, or where he was living.

Now he had a decision to make.

Should he go after Windom and Creek or after the two men who were trailing Abby?

There was no decision to make, really. If Abby was in danger, she was his most urgent assignment.

"Do you know the names of the two men who you think were following Miss Abby?" he asked Sammy.

"Yep. I don't know their last names, but Lou was one and Pat the other. They're riding tan geldings, and both horses have a white blaze on their muzzles. I think one of them chews tobacco twists. I seen him at the Hoot Owl more'n once with Cordwainer and several of his men who got here of an evenin'."

"Thanks, Sammy. You've been a big help. Now doctor those cuts on your head and take some powders if you need them."

"I will, Mr. Slocum. And I'll hold your room for you."

Slocum left and walked to the stables.

Alvaro seemed to have been waiting for him. Slocum was surprised to see that he had Ferro in a stall, all saddled and bridled.

"What's this about, Alvaro?" Slocum asked.

"Ah, I think you need your horse, John. Two men came by here this morning and asked if you were in town."

"Two men? Cordwainer's men?"

Alvaro nodded.

"They wanted to see if your horse was there, but I told them you had left last night. I hid Ferro in a stall and they couldn't see him."

"Who were the men? Do you know?"

"I know. One was Joe Creek. The other was Cory Windom. They started to get mean and I picked up a pitchfork and they backed out."

"Do you think they believed you?"

"I do not know. They were mad and told me that if they found out I was lying, they would make me sorry I was alive."

"Do you have a pistol or a shotgun, Alvaro?"

Alvaro grinned.

"I have a pistol, a little one, in my pocket, and I have a scattergun in the tack room. I am not afraid of those two."

"Well, you'd better be careful when you go home tonight or when you're out in the open."

"I know. They are back-shooters. I will be careful. I am careful all the time. This town can be a bad place sometimes, John. Men are shot and others are hanged. One must always be careful."

"I'll be riding out," Slocum said as he entered the stall. He slung his saddlebags in back of the cantle, attached his rifle and scabbard to his saddle, and tied on his bedroll over Ferro's rump. "You take care, Alvaro."

"You take care also, John Slocum."

Slocum rode out of the rear of the stable and took a roundabout path past the arrastre, and into the timber. He saw the tracks of Abby's dun horse and then the tracks of the men who were following her.

It was going to be hard tracking through the timber and deadfalls of the mountainous terrain. He knew that Abby was very careful and never rode the same trail twice when she went to see Wally. He was surprised, a half hour later, when he saw one of the tracking outlaws' horses break off and leave the other to follow Abby's trail.

Now, he did have a decision to make.

Why did one rider break off and leave only one to follow Abby?

He would have to sort it out.

Did one of the men return to town? He had to find out.

He rode off some distance to follow the breakaway rider's tracks. They did not turn and head back to town. Instead the tracks angled almost parallel to Abby's, as if he was trying to get ahead of her.

Or maybe, he thought, they meant to box her in and kidnap her.

Either way, he began to feel a sense of dread. Abby was in danger and he had two men to deal with, one following her, the other unseen, somewhere in the thick timber, perhaps waiting in ambush for Abby.

He rode on, following the one set of tracks, his uneasiness growing with each twist and turn. Then he saw where Abby had veered off and was riding out of the timber, onto a flat that was strewn with large boulders and limestone outcroppings that looked like the ruins of old temples in some ancient land. The limestone was overgrown with bushes and flocked with moss. The going was very tough, up and down, around natural obstacles, with the only sound the crunch of dead pine needles under Ferro's hooves.

The outlaw's horse left scuff marks in the ground. It dragged its left hind foot every few feet. So that horse was easy to track. Abby's horse left faint impressions on bare ground, but otherwise, she seemed to be holding to ground that would help mask her tracks.

Smart gal, Slocum thought.

But where was she going? Did she know she had at least one man on her trail?

He noticed that she never stopped, but kept riding into more difficult terrain, and it was impossible to see more than a few yards in any direction because of the tall pines and the firs and spruce that grew thick among the junipers. Plenty of deer tracks there, too, and he saw where a bear had stood and scraped a blaze on one of the pines. He could smell bear scat and so could Ferro, who snorted and sidestepped every mound of offal.

Then, higher up, he saw the tracks of the other horse. They crossed ahead of Abby's and her tracker's since her tracks covered his.

Something was up, Slocum knew.

He stopped to listen, hoping to hear the sounds of horses up ahead.

There was nothing but silence.

And the silence filled him with a deep dread.

Where was Abby?

Should he put Ferro to a gallop and ride blindly ahead to warn her or blow the two outlaws to kingdom come?

If he did that, he might get them both killed before he could even see one of her pursuers, much less get off a shot.

He prodded Ferro's flanks with his blunt spurs and started back up the trail that wasn't a trail.

It was then that he heard a scream.

The scream was full of terror and it was a woman's scream.

Abby's scream.

20

Soon after Abby left the town and entered the timber, she mentally chose a path to Wally's cabin. It was one that she had never taken before since it led through part of Union Flat, the most rugged part. She had been there once before and had marveled at the size of the huge boulders and the strange limestone formations that seemed to grow out of the high ridges and made her feel as if an advanced race of humans had once lived there and built temples and buildings that had since decayed.

She chose that circuitous path because she was concerned, more than ever, about being followed. Why had Constable Mayfair been watching her in town? What interest could he have in her? And there were other matters that gave her worry. At least two of Cordwainer's men were in town at an early hour. She was used to being the only person on the street when Arnie Canby opened his store, and that was only when he was expecting the supply wagon from San Bernardino.

No, something was up and she couldn't put a finger on it. Mayfair might have been reporting her movements to Cordwainer or to some of his men. Now that Slocum, her Johnnie, was in Halcyon Valley, and had killed Hutch, it seemed to her that his presence had stirred up a hornet's nest.

She relied on Choc, her dun gelding, to check her back trail. The horse had keen hearing and an amazing sense of smell. More than once, Choc, short for Chocolate, had warned her of men on her trail. He would turn his head and look off in different directions when she was being followed, and she had been able to backtrack or circle to avoid any follower that Choc detected.

Choc was particularly nervous that morning, she noticed. He would perk his ears into twisting cones and his nostrils would quiver whenever he looked at their back trail.

"What is it, Choc?" she whispered at one point.

Choc whickered softly.

She rode to higher ground, but did not stop. She kept looking back over her shoulder, and Choc was looking back and all around. She patted his withers and stroked his short mane.

She did not want to turn back. She was desperate to see Wally, and he could use the groceries she was bringing.

Just before she reached Wally's cabin, a man came riding out of the brush straight toward her.

He grabbed Choc's bridle and jerked the reins from her hand.

Abby screamed, but another man came up from behind and jerked her out of the saddle. He clamped his hand over her mouth.

"You holler once more, lady, and I'll cold-cock you,"

the man growled as he laid her flat on the ground and again covered her mouth with his hand.

"You got her, Lou," Pat said, holding on to her horse as it sidestepped and kicked both hind legs into the air.

"Dump those saddlebags and control that dun, Pat," Lou said. "I'm gonna gag this little gal and tie her hands behind her back."

Lou stripped his bandanna from his neck and covered Abby's mouth. He wrapped the cloth around her head and tied it tight in a double knot. Then he grabbed some manila clothesline from his back pocket, flipped her over on her stomach, and bound her hands together.

Pat dumped her saddlebags to the ground and whopped her horse hard on the nose. Choc stopped trying to run away and stood there, wheezing slightly.

"Lou, they's a cabin down there. I reckon that's her brother's."

"Cut some blazes on these trees with your knife, Pat, and let's get the hell out of here."

Pat grabbed the trailing reins and led Choc to several trees. He slashed bark off the pines and then rode back to help Lou.

Lou lifted Abby up by her armpits.

"Can you get her in the saddle, Lou?" Pat asked.

"If she don't go willin', I'll cold-cock her and hog-tie her to the saddle," Lou said.

He poked Abby in the back with his fist and shoved her toward Choc.

"Get up," he ordered.

Shaking from head to toe, Abby lifted one leg and her foot found the stirrup. Lou pushed on her butt until she was seated.

"Now you just sit real still, Abigail," Lou said. "We ain't goin' to hurt you. Just take you for a little ride."

She said something beneath the gag, but it was muffled and unintelligible.

"Watch her, Pat, while I straddle my horse," Lou said.

He climbed up into the saddle. Then he rode toward the blazed trees and looked down at the log cabin some three hundred yards away. There was no sign of life, but he was pretty sure her brother was inside. And he hadn't heard Abby scream.

He turned his horse.

"Know where we are, Pat?" he asked as he rode up alongside.

"I been keepin' track. We're at one end of Union Flat, I reckon. If we ride due east, we ought to find Cordwainer."

"Head on out, then. I'll ride drag on our prisoner. You just lead her horse, and if she tries to jump down, I'll lay a rifle butt across the back of her pretty head."

Pat rode off through the timber and the boulders.

Lou kept checking his back trail to make sure they weren't being followed.

"That was easy," he said later to Pat.

"Piece of cake," Pat said.

Abby shook inside with rage. How could she have been so foolish? She had led those men to within a stone's throw of Wally's cabin.

He would never forgive her.

If she lived.

21

Slocum rode up on the site of Abby's abduction a few minutes later. He saw the fresh knife blazes on the trees, the dumped saddlebags with canned goods and vegetables strewn on the ground. He saw the moil of tracks and signs of the struggle.

He wondered, though, about the fresh blazes.

He rode over to the pines and then, out of the corner of his eye, saw the log cabin a few hundred yards away.

He cursed under his breath.

He debated whether to follow the three sets of horse tracks or ride down to the cabin.

Two heads were better than one, he decided. and turned Ferro to the downslope.

"Hello, the cabin," he called when he was within fifty yards. A thin column of blue smoke streamed upward from the chimney. "Wally, I'm riding your way."

A moment later a man stepped out of the cabin, a rifle in his hands.

It was Wally.

"That you, John?"

"It's me and we got trouble, Wally."

He rode down and dismounted.

"You have a horse close by?" Slocum asked.

"Sure. Why?"

"They got Abby," Slocum said. He raised his arm and pointed up the slope toward the timber. "I guess you didn't hear her scream."

"Hell no, I didn't. Who got her?"

"Two of Cordwainer's men. Looks like they followed her and jumped her up yonder. Maybe tied her up and gagged her since I didn't hear her scream but once."

"*Damn!*" Wally exploded. "Can we catch them?"

"I don't know if we can catch them, but we can sure as hell track them. They rode off before I got here."

"I won't be long," Wally said and raced toward the cabin. He leaned his rifle against the door and then ran in back of the cabin and into a copse of trees. Slocum followed.

Wally had built a pole corral and a shelter for a water trough, hay bin, and room enough for two horses. As Slocum watched, Wally bridled his horse, slapped a blanket on its back, then a single-cinch saddle.

"Be just a minute."

"Better strap on a pistol, Wally, and pack that rifle, plenty of ammunition. We could ride into a fight."

"Hold my horse," Wally said as he swung out of the saddle and handed his reins to Slocum.

In a few minutes, Wally reemerged from the cabin. He wore a gun belt and holster, carried a rifle scabbard.

He picked up his rifle and attached the scabbard to his saddle. He mounted up and shoved the rifle into its sheath.

"Where now?" he asked.

"Follow me," Slocum said.

The two men rode up to the place where Abby had been overpowered and captured.

"Do you read sign, Wally?" Slocum asked.

"Not nearly as good as you, John. But I can see that this is where they got Abby."

He dismounted and picked up the oversized saddlebags. As Slocum studied the tracks, Wally began picking up the canned goods, celery stalks, carrots, and string beans. He slung the saddlebags onto his horse's rump and climbed back into the saddle.

"She didn't have a chance," Slocum said. "One rider came busting out of the brush and probably grabbed her horse's bridle. The other came up from behind and looks like he knocked her out of the saddle. See those smudges where a small body was lying and then turned over?"

"I just see that the ground is disturbed," Wally said. His hat rode a little on one side as he scratched above his ear.

"Tracks tell the story," Slocum said.

"Now what?"

Slocum pointed toward the east.

"That's the direction they took. They won't be riding fast. Maybe we can catch up to them."

"They're going down to where Union Flat levels off," Wally said. "That's where Cordwainer has his cabin. It's well protected and he always has a few men with rifles guarding his place."

"Can't be helped," Slocum said. "No telling what

Cordwainer will do to Abby to make her tell him where your mine is."

Wally cursed under his breath.

They began to follow the horse tracks through heavy timber and around huge boulders and the limestone outcroppings.

Slocum had no trouble deciphering the tracks. He determined that one rider was leading Abby's horse. She rode in the middle of the trio, with one rider bringing up the rear. They were not trying to conceal their tracks, but were keeping their horses at a brisk trot.

Slocum figured that they had at least a half-hour's lead, maybe more, and no matter how close or far it was to Cordwainer's cabin, they had little chance of catching up to the outlaws. The land was too rugged and they had to jump over large deadfalls and skirt massive boulders.

These problems were compounded by the fact that the two men knew where they were going and Slocum did not.

"Do you know how far it is to Cordwainer's place?" Slocum asked.

"Union Flat is pretty big and he's on the far end of it. We're not even down to flat land yet. It's a bitchwilly going through here."

"Tell me about it," Slocum said.

The two men did not talk for several minutes.

Then they descended onto even terrain. The trees were still thick, but there were several game trails that Slocum spotted. Squirrels scampered up trees ahead of them, and Ferro shied at a timber rattler as it coiled up on a log and shook its rattles.

"Not far now, John," Wally said. "Maybe a mile or so."

"Still, we can't catch them. They've got too much of a lead and they were running at a fast trot."

"You can tell all that from their tracks?"

"Yes. Abby's on her horse. Probably tied up and gagged so that she can't cry out. These men are bastards."

"I know they are," Wally said. "Now I wonder how we're going to get Abby back. Cordwainer's liable to shoot her just to get back at me."

"We'll have to give it some thought when the time comes," Slocum said.

Presently, Wally stuck out his arm and grabbed Slocum's sleeve.

"Hold up," he said, his voice nearly a whisper.

Slocum reined Ferro to a halt.

Wally pulled up alongside him and reined his horse to a halt.

"His cabin is just up ahead," Wally whispered. "See all those big boulders?"

"I see the rocks, but no cabin."

"Just beyond them is his place. John, he's got gun ports, men prowling around outside. We don't stand a chance against him and his men. And they'll sure as hell be waiting for us."

Slocum said nothing for several moments.

"Maybe we can get Abby back without any gunplay," he said.

"How? Do you have a plan?"

"I don't know if it will work or not, but it might. It will take some nerve."

"Well, you have more nerve than anybody I know, John. Me, I'm plumb scared to death that something will happen to Abby."

"I am, too," Slocum said.

"You're scared?"

"Not scared, Wally. Just a little on edge. But I do have a plan. It's a small one and might not work. But it's all I can think of."

"What's your plan, John?"

"Cordwainer is a greedy man, is he not?"

"Yes. He's greedy and he's meaner than a he-bear, without a whit of conscience."

"Then that's how we get Abby back."

"I don't follow you, John."

"Just play along, then, Wally. Let me handle the palaver with Cordwainer."

"His men probably have orders to shoot you on sight."

Slocum gave out a low chuckle.

"They might shoot me, Wally, but I'm betting they won't shoot you. Cordwainer wants your mine. He can't get it from a dead man."

"What? You want me to go up there—"

"Settle down, Wally. Let me handle it. But if I open the ball, be prepared to shoot the first of his men you see."

"I—I don't know, John. Gunfighting is way out of my line of work."

"You'd be surprised what a man can do when the chips are down and his back is against the wall."

"I hope you know what you're doing, John."

"I hope so, too," Slocum said and tapped Ferro on the flanks.

The two men rode slowly into what Wally would call the "jaws of death."

And that's just what those huge boulders looked like: massive jaws. And beyond, the unknown, a veritable snake den of ruthless killers.

He and Wally were riding right into the most dangerous spot on earth.

Slocum hoped he could pull off his plan.

Otherwise, Cordwainer would have two more notches
on his gun and there would be two more graves in Halcyon Valley.

22

Bud Rafferty was perched atop a large boulder, his Winchester rifle in his lap. He smoked a cigarette he had rolled moments before. He listened to every forest sound. He peered in every direction. A pair of U.S. Army field glasses hung from a strap around his neck.

Every so often Bud lifted the binoculars to his eyes and scanned the flat beyond the piles of boulders. He waved to Claude Wicks, who was circling Cordwainer's cabin, his rifle resting on his shoulder, military style.

"Pretty quiet," Claude said.

"Jess up yet?"

"Yep. He's had his coffee and is goin' over the books."

"Well, he's got a lot to tally, I reckon," Bud said and waved again as Claude continued his patrol.

Ten minutes later, Bud spotted movement beyond a phalanx of boulders. He stood up and put the binoculars to his face and adjusted the lenses. Then he called down to Claude in a loud voice.

"Friend or foe?" Claude asked.

"Dunno yet," Bud replied.

Three minutes later, he breathed a sigh of relief.

"It's Lou and Pat," he told Claude. "Better call out Jess. They got a gal with 'em. Looks like it could be the Newman woman."

Claude rapped on the cabin door.

"Boss, Bud says he thinks Lou and Pat are ridin' up with that Abby Newman."

Cordwainer looked up at Bud.

"You sure, Bud?" he asked.

"Certain sure, Jess. They got her sandwiched atwixt 'em. She's on that dun horse."

"Well, keep an eye on them. Make sure there's nobody following them."

Five minutes later, Lou and Pat rode up with Abby. Both wore wide grins on their faces.

"We got her, boss," Pat said.

"And we know where her brother's cabin is," Lou said.

"Light down," Cordwainer said, "and bring the gal inside. I want to know all that you know and what she knows."

He went back into the cabin as the two men dismounted and dragged Abby from her saddle. They did not untie her, but shoved her into the cabin as if she were a criminal in custody.

"We know right where Wally Newman lives," Lou said. "We blazed some trees so's we can find it again."

"Give Miss Abby a chair and untie her," Cordwainer ordered. "That ain't no way to treat a lady."

Pat untied the bonds around Abby's wrists. He sat

her in a chair. She glared at Cordwainer as she rubbed her wrists. The rope had left impressions in her flesh.

"Ain't you goin' to thank me, Miss Abby?" Cordwainer said.

"Thank you for what? Your men knocked me out of my saddle and tied me up."

"Well, were you heading for Wally's?"

"That's none of your business," she said.

"Oh, I think it is. I want to know where his mine is and where he filed his claim."

"Well, you'll never find out either one," she said.

"We have ways of getting information from folks," Cordwainer said. "Especially from young, smart-mouthed women."

Abby said nothing.

There was a silence in the room for several seconds.

Finally, Lou Jessup spoke up. "Do we get our hunnert dollars, Jess?" he asked.

"Yeah," Pat said. "We did what you wanted."

Cordwainer turned his attention to the two men who stood behind Abby.

"You'll get your money in good time. Now go on outside and have a smoke or a chew. I want to talk to Miss Abby by herself."

"Okay, boss," Lou said.

The two men left the room and closed the door.

"All I want, Miss Abby, is a little information. Now we know where your brother lives. You can keep him alive and unhurt if you tell me what I want to know. Where is his gold mine and where did he file his claim?"

"I'll never tell," she said. "You can kill me or torture me, but I won't betray my brother."

"What about this Slocum? Is he your sweetie?"

"You have a way of fouling the name of everyone I

care about," she said. "You make Wally and Johnnie sound like filth in your mouth."

Cordwainer smiled, but it was not a mirthful smile. It was a smug, noncaring smile.

He got up and walked over to her. He looked down and she looked up.

"If we have to hunt your brother down and put a hot poker to his eyes, you'll hear him scream for mercy."

"Johnnie Slocum will kill you first," she said.

"I've got men hot on his trail right now, little lady. He'll be wolf meat by tomorrow."

"You don't know Slocum," she said.

"No, but you do. I wonder if we can't use you as bait to draw that bastard out in the open."

She spat at Cordwainer.

Her spit struck him in the crotch. He looked down at the liquid substance.

"My patience is running a mite thin, Miss Abby."

"As if I cared a hoot or a holler," she said.

"Maybe I won't torture you," he said as he turned away and sat down at his table. "Maybe I'll just take you to my bed tonight and put the boots to you."

Abby knew what the expression meant. He was threatening to rape her.

But she would not give Cordwainer the satisfaction of responding to his threat. She just sat there and quietly glared at him.

Before either of them spoke again, they heard a commotion outside.

There was a knock on the door.

"Who is it?" Cordwainer demanded. He was plainly irritated.

"It's me, Pat. Bud says somebody's comin'. Might be Slocum and Newman."

"I'll be right out," Cordwainer said.

Then he walked over to Abby and grabbed her by both wrists and jerked her to her feet.

"Come on," he said. "If that's Slocum and he's come for you, you'll be the first to die, you little bitch."

She struggled to free herself from Cordwainer's grip, but he was too strong. He dragged her from the cabin and stood with her just outside the door. Lou and Pat stood by Bud's sentinel post atop the pile of boulders. All three men were staring off in the distance in the same direction the two men and Abby had come from several moments before.

"What is it, Bud?"

"They's two riders a-comin', near as I can figger,' he said. "They're comin' mighty slow."

"Do you recognize them? Who in hell are they?" Cordwainer demanded.

"Can't see too well. One of 'em's on a black horse. Dressed in black, too."

"Hell, that's Slocum," Lou said.

"Maybe," Bud said.

"Hell yes, it's Slocum. And Newman's probably with him."

"Well, don't any of you shoot lessen I order you to," Cordwainer said. "This might be our chance to kill two birds with one stone. I've got Newman's sister, and if they want her bad enough, they'll have to talk mighty fast."

Lou and Pat smiled and exchanged glances. They seemed proud of their boss.

"You bastard," Abby whispered under her breath.

"They're still a-comin', boss," Bud said. "Slow as molasses in January."

"Good," Cordwainer said and drew his pistol. He

cocked the .44 and put the barrel against Abby's temple. "Let 'em come."

Abby's knees turned to jelly and she felt faint. She strained to see if it really was her brother and Johnnie, but she could see only boulders and trees. She summoned up her courage and strength, and her knees returned to normal. She waited, holding her breath until it turned to fire in her lungs.

The barrel of the pistol was cold against her flesh.

She was certain, then, that Cordwainer would hold to his promise and shoot her dead if Wally and Johnnie made a move to free her from this mad man.

She began to pray silently, but the words were all jumbled and meaningless in her mind.

The waiting was agony.

23

Even though both Slocum and Newman were anxious to find Abby, they rode at a slow pace through the timber. The tracks of the three horses were easy for Slocum to follow, and Wally knew where Cordwainer's cabin was, so they made good time.

Along the way, Slocum outlined his plan to Wally.

"You have to do it, Wally," Slocum said.

"Anything to get Abby away from that bastard, Cordwainer," he said. "But I don't like it none."

"No, I didn't expect you would," Slocum said.

"In fact, the more I think about what you want me to do, the less I like it."

"Sometimes," Slocum said, "you have to trust someone. Like when your daddy tells you to jump off the barn and he'll catch you."

"Or telling me to jump in the water when I can't swim. My pa did that. 'You won't drown,' he said, and

I believed him. But, John, I swallowed a hell of a lot of water learning to swim."

Slocum chuckled.

"Well, you might have to swallow something worse than water when we brace Cordwainer."

"Is that a threat, John, or a warning?"

Slocum laughed.

"Maybe both," he said.

The men rode on and it seemed an eternity to Slocum. The tracks of the horses they were following showed him that the men he tracked were not running hard, but kept their horses at a slow, steady pace. At times, they had stopped, to reconnoiter, Slocum imagined, because the horses changed directions slightly.

"You could get lost in here," Slocum said. "Real easy."

"And men get lost in these mountains all the time," Wally said. "Some are never found until someone comes across their skeletons."

"I've been in such places before," Slocum said.

Finally, Wally slowed his pace and leaned over toward Slocum to whisper what was on his mind.

"See all those big boulders?" he asked.

Slocum nodded.

"We're getting close. Damned close."

"Just let me know when you spot Cordwainer's cabin. I don't want to ride up there and get shot out of the saddle."

"I will. He'll have a lookout sitting or standing atop one of those big boulders. "He'll probably see us before we get a good look at him."

"Remember to let me do the talking, Wally."

"It's your call, John. I do trust you."

"Good," Slocum said.

A little later, Wally whispered, "We're getting damned close. Should see the lookout pretty soon."

Wally reined his horse up and kept him at a very slow walk. Slocum did the same.

They slipped through the pines and spruce, angling through shafts of sunlight that danced with dust motes, their horses' hooves stepping on dried pine needles that shone like amber jewels.

Slocum's hand went to his belt buckle and he tucked in his shirt, pushing something behind it from one position to another. Wally caught the movement and looked at Slocum hard for a long second.

"Get a wood tick, John?" he asked.

"Belly gun. I just want it right behind my buckle so it doesn't show."

"A belly gun? What for? What kind is it?"

"It's a Remington .38. And it's just in case."

"In case of what?" Wally asked.

Slocum shrugged and assumed an air of nonchalance.

"Sometimes, when you least expect it, someone will get the drop on you. You can't draw your sidearm. So if that happens, you might be able to reach down and get the belly gun and turn the tables on your attacker."

"Well, I damned sure hope that doesn't happen when we come to getting Abby away from Cordwainer."

"I hope so, too," Slocum said.

A few moments later, Wally pointed to a jumble of rocks, large boulders that seemed to have been piled up in a heap by some giant force.

"There's Bud Rafferty," he said. "One of Cordwainer's men. Sittin' atop that boulder yonder. And he's lookin' straight at us."

Slocum craned his neck and looked through the

trees. There was a man whose head was turned in their direction. As they watched, he put a pair of binoculars to his eyes.

"He's spotted us, I think," Wally said.

"No doubt."

Slocum raised a hand and pulled a white handkerchief from his back pocket. Then he stood up in the stirrups, drew his knife, and cut a small limb from one of the pines. He shaved off the little branches and tied the handkerchief to the slender end.

"You goin' to surrender, John?" Wally asked.

"This might tell them that I come in peace." Slocum waved the makeshift flag and grinned. "I'll be lying, of course," he said.

They rode through the trees and halted their horses just short of the nearest pile of boulders.

"You there," Slocum called. "We've come to see Jess Cordwainer. Just to talk. We don't want any trouble."

Bud stood up and looked down at Cordwainer.

"Let 'em come in, but every one of you draw your pistols or point your rifles at both men, and if either of them so much as twitches, you blow 'em clean out of their saddles."

"Yeah, boss," Lou said as he drew his pistol. Pat drew his, too, and Bud raised his rifle to his shoulder.

"Come on in," Bud called. "Real slow and keep your hands where I can see 'em."

Both John and Wally raised their hands and spurred their horses onward at a slow walk.

John kept the handkerchief floating high over his head.

"You can drop the hanky, mister," Bud said. "Ride right on in until I tell you to stop."

Slocum dropped the stick with his handkerchief tied to it. He and Wally rode to a point where they could see Cordwainer holding a big .44 Remington to Abby's head, and two men pointing pistols at them. Both pistols were cocked.

"That's far enough," Bud said after Cordwainer nodded to him.

"Well, well, well," Cordwainer said. "What do we have here? Wally Newman and his gunny friend who's wanted for murder. I suppose you know I hold all the cards in this deal."

"We know," Slocum said. "We want a new deck. We've come to bargain with you."

Cordwainer looked surprised.

"Bargain with me?"

"That's what I said, Cordwainer. You have Miss Abby, and Wally here has a producing gold mine. He's willing to sign his mine over to you if you give us Abby."

There was a long silence as Cordwainer stared at Slocum in disbelief.

"You serious, Newman?"

Wally just nodded. Slocum had asked him to keep quiet and that was what he was doing.

"He's serious," Slocum said. "His sister means more to him than all the gold in the world. If you turn her over to us, he's going to draw you a map to his mine and he will sign off his claim to you. No strings. Straight deal."

"Well, I'm damned sure interested in such a deal," Cordwainer said.

"You give us Abby and you've got yourself a working gold mine," Slocum said. "Lock, stock, and barrel."

"Light down, then, one at a time. You first, Slocum and no tricky moves. Then you step down, Wally."

Slocum dismounted.

"Drop your gun belt," Cordwainer ordered.

Slocum unbuckled his cartridge belt and let his holster drop to the ground. He held both hands high.

"Now, Wally," Cordwainer said, "you do the same. Real slow-like."

Wally stepped out of his saddle. He unbuckled his gun belt and let the pistol touch the ground before he released the cartridge belt. He raised his hands.

"Come on inside, you two," he said. "Lou, you and Pat keep your guns on them."

Then Cordwainer pulled his pistol away, and eased the hammer down to half-cock and holstered the .44. He pushed Abby in front of him and entered the cabin.

All of them walked into the cabin's front room. Cordwainer waved Wally and Slocum to the table and put Abby in a straight-backed chair a few feet away where he could keep an eye on her.

"Sit down, boys," Cordwainer said. He pulled up a chair. "Lou, in that desk over there, you'll find some sheet paper, an inkwell, and a quill pen. Bring 'em over to the table. Pat, you keep on eye on our three visitors. If either of these men so much as lift their asses up to fart, you shoot the gal first and then turn your gun on them two."

"Right, boss," Pat said.

Lou went to the small rolltop desk against the wall and opened a drawer. He took out several sheets of white paper, then lifted the ink bottle from its well and a quill pen from one of the cubbyholes. He brought them to the table and laid them in front of Cordwainer.

"You stand by the door, Lou, and keep an eye on Slocum, Newman, and Miss Abby."

"Sure will, Jess," Lou said. He stood by the open door and moved the barrel of his pistol back and forth between Abby, Wally, and Slocum.

"Now, then," Cordwainer said, "where do you want to start? You want to draw me a map showin' me where your mine is, or a paper transferrin' ownership to your claim?"

Slocum nodded to Wally, indicating that he should answer Cordwainer.

"Whichever you prefer, Jess," Wally said.

"Draw the map," Cordwainer said. "Then I'll tell you what to write."

"Damned mine's about petered out anyways," Wally said as he dipped the pen into the ink bottle.

Slocum kicked him under the table.

"What's that?" Cordwainer said. "Are you lyin' to me?"

"I reckon I was. I hate to lose that mine. I think we're close to finding the mother lode. A few more feet. I'm into a rich vein and it keeps getting wider with every swing of the pick."

Cordwainer's face cracked in a wide smile.

"Your map better be right, Wally," he said.

"It's in a straight line from my cabin and the Ettinger mine," Wally said. "Easy to find once you know where it is."

"It better be," Cordwainer said.

Slocum watched as Wally drew a crude map on one of the papers. He drew a square where his cabin was, then a line to his mine, and beyond, another square, which he labeled ETTINGER MINE.

Wally passed the map over to Cordwainer, sliding it across the pinewood table.

Cordwainer looked at it then slid another blank sheet over to Wally.

"I'll tell you what to write, Wally," he said. "Then you'll sign the paper and my men will witness it."

"I'm not signing a damned thing until you turn Abby over to Slocum here," Wally said.

The room filled up with silence.

Even Slocum was surprised at what Wally said. He hadn't expected it.

He looked at Wally and saw the steely look in his eyes as he stared at Cordwainer.

Cordwainer's jaw hardened to granite and his eyes narrowed to cold slits.

Then he looked at Slocum, whose face was without expression.

"This your idea, Slocum?" Cordwainer asked.

Slocum shook his head.

"Well, it's a piss-poor idea, Wally."

"I'm not signing any paper until I know my sister is safe. And I trust my friend John Slocum. You hand her over and let them leave and then I'll write out the terms and sign your damned paper."

There was another silence. This was deeper and longer lasting than the first one.

Everyone in the room seemed frozen, immobile, as if they were wooden mannequins.

Then Cordwainer rose from his chair and pulled his pistol from its holster. He walked over to Abby, put the barrel up to her throat, and cocked the hammer back all the way.

Slocum glared at him, but was powerless to move. He had two guns on him and both Lou and Pat were as twitchy as a pair of nervous squirrels. They were just itching to blast him to pieces with their bullets.

The tension in the room was like a steel spring attached to a box of explosive powder. One false move from anyone could set it off and blow them all clean to hell.

24

Abby closed her eyes as she felt the icy iron of the gun barrel touch her throat. She squeezed both lids tight.

Slocum felt the volcano of his anger rising inside his gut, the first tremors in his lungs. He wanted to jump up, grab Cordwainer by the throat, and squeeze his neck until his spine cracked, his eyes bulged out, and blood squirted from his mouth and nose. Slocum's green eyes flashed a viridian fire as he controlled his rage.

Then he reached out with his left hand and grabbed the blank piece of paper from under Wally's pen poised like a dagger above it.

He crumpled the paper in his hands.

"You shoot Abby, Cordwainer, and you'll never get anything from Wally Newman," Slocum said. Each word was measured. Each word carried weight. Each word was filled with poisonous barbs.

Cordwainer blinked.

He opened his mouth as if to curse Slocum or say something in rebuttal, but no sound came out.

Instead, he swallowed hard and the pistol in his hand glided away from Abby's throat.

Slocum heard the slide of the hammer as Cordwainer pulled it to half-cock. The converted Remington .44 looked like a dead sash weight in Cordwainer's hands as he slid it back in his holster. He walked slowly back to the table, looked down at Slocum, his face contorted into lines and wrinkles until it looked like boiled mutton, steaming in a seething pot with flames licking the bottom.

Cordwainer sat down and picked up another sheet of paper, passed it to Wally.

"Write down my terms," he said, "and I promise that all three of you will go free once you sign the mine over to me."

"You won't let Abby go now?" Wally said.

"That would be stupid of me," Cordwainer said. "She's my ace in the hole. My promise is good, I swear."

Wally looked at Slocum.

"Go ahead, Wally," Slocum said. "Write it all out but don't sign it until Cordwainer actually hands Abby over to me."

Wally looked across the table at Cordwainer.

"Go ahead, then, Jess. Tell me what you want me to write down. I guess I have to trust you, for my sister's sake."

"You damned sure do," Cordwainer said.

He began to dictate the transfer of Wally's mine to him.

"What's the mine called in your claim?" he asked when he got to the pertinent clause.

"It's called 'The Lorelei,' after my wife," Wally said.

Abby stiffened in her chair at the mention of her brother's dead wife.

No one saw her reaction except Slocum.

"All right, you hereby deed over to me, Jesse Cordwainer, all rights and title to The Lorelei Mine without encumbrances."

Wally dipped the quill pen into the ink bottle and finished drafting the document. He shoved the paper over to Cordwainer, who spun it around and read it.

"Draw four lines at the bottom and put your name under one of them, my name under another, and the word 'Witness' under the other two." He slid the sheet back to Wally.

Then he turned to look at Pat Morris.

"When we finish signing this, Pat," he said, "you come over and sign as a witness."

Then he looked at Lou.

"Jessup," Cordwainer said, "after Pat signs, you come and sign the other witness line."

Lou nodded in assent.

Wally drew the lines, four of them. They were fairly straight and he wrote under each one according to Cordwainer's wishes.

"There," he said, and signed his name.

Cordwainer took the paper and examined the signature of Wallace Newman. Then, with a wry smile, he signed his name. He blew the ink dry and held up the paper and waved it as if it were a fan.

Then he beckoned to Pat, who walked over and holstered his pistol. He flexed his arm and picked up the pen. He signed his name. His hand moved painfully slow as he looped the letters. Then he stepped back.

"That okay, boss?" he asked.

"You could get a job writing prescriptions for doctors, Pat," Cordwainer said.

Then he looked at Jessup.

"Lou? Come here and sign this."

Lou holstered his pistol and walked to the table.

He had a sheepish look on his face.

"I ain't never learnt to write," he told Cordwainer.

"You dumb sonofabitch," Cordwainer said and waved him away.

He looked out through the open door.

"Bud," he called, "can you write your damned name?"

Bud stepped up to the door, his rifle still in his hands.

"Sure, boss. I ain't too good at it, but—"

"Then, get your fat ass in here and sign this here document. Put the rifle by the door."

Bud came inside and leaned his rifle against the wall next to the door. He waddled over to the table.

"Where do you want me to sign?" he asked.

"That blank line down at the bottom," Cordwainer said. "Bud, can you read?"

"Not too good," he said, "but my ma taught me how to write my name."

"Sign on that line. And don't put no X there."

Cordwainer put his index finger on the blank line, then took it away as Bud bent over to sign his name. He was left-handed.

As he bent over, his pistol was right next to Slocum's face. He gave a sidelong glance at both Jessup and Morris. Both of their pistols were still in their holsters.

He would never have a better chance, Slocum thought.

Still, it was four against one, and both Wally and Abby were exposed and without any weapons for protection.

He would have to be fast. Faster than he had ever been.

And there was still one man on guard outside. He glanced through the door and saw the man climb to the top stone in the pile of boulders where Bud had been.

Bud began to write his name in a long lazy scrawl.

The butt of his pistol jutted from its holster so close that Slocum could smell the oil on the barrel. It was a converted Colt Navy, probably .36 caliber.

Now or never, he thought and his hand was a striking viper, lightning fast.

He jerked the Colt from the holster, and shoved Bud into Cordwainer. He cocked the pistol on the rise and shot Lou in the belly. Then he swung the pistol at Pat, who was pulling on his pistol. He shot him between the eyes.

Cordwainer flailed his arms under the weight of the heavyset Bud as Slocum rose up and cold-cocked Rafferty with the butt of the Navy, knocking him cold. Bud slumped down on Cordwainer, whose eyes were frantic.

Just then, they all heard a rifle shot from outside.

Slocum turned and looked up at the man on the rock. Blood streamed from his face as he toppled over and fell to the ground, his rifle rattling against the rocks.

Pat groaned in agony a few feet away, his belly gushing blood. Lou lay dead-eyed, a black hole in the center of his forehead.

Abby screamed in terror.

Wally scooted his chair back and ran to the door. He picked up Bud's rifle, cocked it, and shot Pat in the throat. His moan wound up as a bloody gurgle.

Then they all heard hoofbeats outside.

Someone was riding up mighty fast.

Cordwainer shoved Bud off his chest and clawed for his pistol.

Time seemed to freeze that one moment for an eternity.

There was the smell of burnt powder, and wisps of smoke hung in the air like a fog over dank swamp waters with its floating dead.

25

The hoofbeats outside ceased abruptly.

Slocum cocked Bud's Navy and fired point-blank at Cordwainer.

The gun misfired and jammed.

He threw it at Cordwainer, who jerked his head out of the way.

Slocum's right hand went to his belt and slid inside his pants. He pulled out the belly gun, cocked it just as Cordwainer was raising his pistol to cock it and fire at Slocum.

A cloud passed over Cordwainer's eyes as he realized he wasn't going to get off a shot.

Slocum squeezed the trigger. The barrel of the Remington belly gun exploded in flame and smoke.

The .38 projectile smashed into Cordwainer's chest. He gasped in pain and blood spurted from the black hole. Whitish lung matter leaked through the wound.

"Bastard," Cordwainer muttered. Blood bubbled out

of his mouth and his gun hand dropped with a thud as the barrel struck the floor.

"So long, Cordwainer," Slocum said as he stepped over to the man and put the barrel of the .38 square at a spot just below Cordwainer's hairline.

He squeezed the trigger and the clouds over Cordwainer's eyes glazed over into a frosty pallor. He fell back, stone dead.

Ruben Vallejo and Elisando Gonzalez entered the cabin. They carried rifles and looked ready to fire.

"It's all over," Wally told them.

They both grinned. Abby ran to her brother and embraced him.

"You do not come to the mine," Ruben said. "So we go to your cabin to look for you. We see your horse is gone and we see the tracks. We see many tracks and we follow them."

"Yes," said Gonzalez. "We follow the tracks and we know where they go. We see your horse and Miss Abby's outside and we shoot the lookout."

The two Mexicans looked around the room in amazement.

"We see your pistols in their holsters outside," Ruben said. "We will get them for you."

The two men left the room and went outside.

Slocum walked over to the table and picked up the document Wally had drawn. He handed it to Wally.

"You might want to use this to start a fire in your fireplace tonight," he said.

Wally laughed, crumpled up the paper, and crammed it into a back pocket.

Abby went to Slocum and put her arms around him. She stood up on tiptoes and kissed him on the lips.

"Oh, Johnnie," she whispered, "I love you so much."

Slocum said not a word, but he kissed her hard and squeezed her even harder against him.

Later, when word got around town that Cordwainer was dead, the constable, along with Cory Windom and Joe Creek, lit a shuck for parts unknown.

Wally had no opposition when he ran for the office of constable and won.

Slocum, as was his custom, drifted away, back down through Jackrabbit Valley.

It was said that Ruby Dawson pined for him so much that she took to drinking and one day she did not wake up, but had died in her sleep.

Wally never did find the mother lode.

But neither did anyone else in Halcyon Valley.

Watch for

SLOCUM AND THE TEXAS TWISTER

404th novel in the exciting SLOCUM series
from Jove

Coming in October!

LONGARM

GIANT-SIZED ADVENTURE FROM AVENGING ANGEL LONGARM.

BY TABOR EVANS

penguin.com/actionwesterns

M456AS05

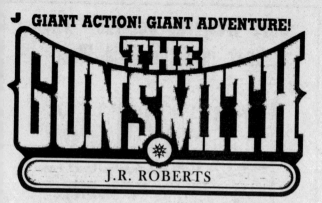

GIANT ACTION! GIANT ADVENTURE!

THE Gunsmith

J.R. ROBERTS

penguin.com/actionwesterns

M455AS0510

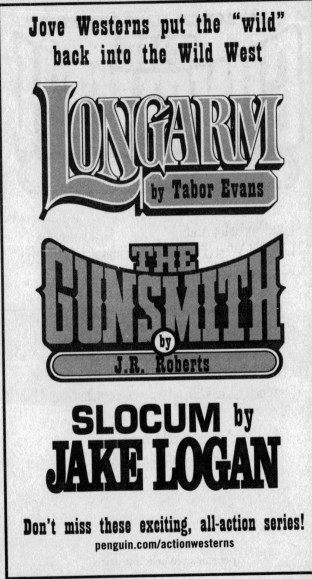